A
SOMETIMES :
E
IMPORTANT A

When John Neufeld's first novel, *Edgar Allan*, appeared, it was hailed by *The New York Times* as "a work of art." The *Times* also selected his second novel, *Lisa, Bright and Dark*, as one of the "outstanding books of the year."

*Now with* Twink *John Neufeld has achieved his most ambitious and unforgettable work of fiction. It is a story of "normal" and "abnormal" people, and the thin line between them. It is the story of the young and the old, reaching to touch each other across the inevitable generation gap. Most of all, it is the story of a "hopeless" girl who managed to keep hope and love alive—in her own heart and the hearts of others . . .*

# Twink

"AN EMOTIONAL SHOCKER . . . INTENSELY REAL"
—*English Journal*

"POIGNANT AND GRIPPING . . . FEW READERS WILL REMAIN UNTOUCHED"
—*Des Moines Register*

# Other SIGNET Titles You Will Enjoy Reading

# ☆ Twink ☆

## (formerly Touching)

•

## A novel
## by

## John Neufeld

A SIGNET BOOK from
NEW AMERICAN LIBRARY
TIMES MIRROR

SIGNET TRADEMARK REG. U.S. PAT. OFF. AND FOREIGN COUNTRIES
REGISTERED TRADEMARK—MARCA REGISTRADA
HECHO EN CHICAGO, U.S.A.

SIGNET, SIGNET CLASSICS, SIGNETTE, MENTOR AND PLUME BOOKS
*are published by The New American Library, Inc.,*
*1301 Avenue of the Americas, New York, New York 10019*

FIRST PRINTING, NOVEMBER, 1971

PRINTED IN THE UNITED STATES OF AMERICA

Two things happened at once: I saw the Volkswagen bus, and I began to sweat. It was hot in the airport, and hotter on the curb. But it wasn't that hot, not even in June. . . .

I walked toward the open doors, ducked my head, kissed my stepmother, Ellie, hello and saw them. I didn't look directly at them. I was just conscious they were there: two wheelchairs locked into the floor of the bus at the back. Two wheelchairs with two scarecrow figures sitting in them, twisted.

My stepmother slid around in her seat and motioned at the pair of girls behind her. "This," she said pointing, "is Twink. And this is one of her friends, Mary Jane. Harry's here now," she said to them.

I had to look then. Just for a second, I had to look straight at them. I tried to smile hello before I realized how dumb that was. Mary Jane's head wasn't turned in my direction, and Twink couldn't even see.

Then I heard the sounds. Sort of chortles, I guess. Almost happy sounds.

And then I felt sick.

Harry Walsh, 16, a rather casual "preppie," meets his stepsister, also 16, for the first time. It rocks him.

And their meeting will shake young readers too. For Harry's world—careless, easy, typical—is as far as it could be from Twink's—troubled, painful, and yet worth it all.

John Neufeld has told Twink's story without tears and flowers, without bright colors and happy endings. It is a gutsy, sometimes shocking but always real tale of a girl who could have been forgotten, and wasn't.

# PART ONE

# Chapter One

Two things happened at once: I saw the Volkswagen bus, and I began to sweat. It was hot in the airport and hotter on the curb. But it wasn't that hot, not even in June.

My father walked ahead with Beau, the man from the Hill. I stopped and took a big breath. Then I followed slowly, glad as I walked closer to the car that I had dark glasses on.

The side doors of the Volks were open so that whatever little breeze there was could circulate. Father stopped and motioned me to come closer. Beau took my suitcases and flung them on the floor of the front seat.

I walked toward the open doors, ducked my head, kissed my stepmother, Ellie, hello and saw them. I didn't look directly at

7

them. I was just conscious they were there: two wheelchairs locked into the floor of the bus at the back. Two wheelchairs with two scarecrow figures sitting in them, twisted.

My stepmother slid around in her seat and motioned at the pair of girls behind her. "This," she said pointing, "is Twink. And this is one of her friends, Mary Jane. Harry's here now," she said to them.

I had to look then. Just for a second, I had to look straight at them. I tried to smile hello before I realized how dumb that was. Mary Jane's head wasn't turned in my direction, and Twink couldn't even see.

Then I heard the sounds. Sort of chortles, I guess. Almost happy sounds.

And then I felt sick.


It wasn't supposed to be this way, I thought. This isn't the way it was supposed to happen.

The bus was on the freeway, heading out toward Christmastree Hill where Twink and Mary Jane and God knew how many other people like them lived. Beau drove carefully and silently, looking only at the road ahead. I was glad of that. I was dripping cold sweat. I didn't want to have to say something polite or funny or interested or anything at all. I looked at my legs, wrapped around my suitcases, twisted uncomfortably and threatening to shake.

Ellie and my father sat in the seat behind me. Sometimes they spoke quietly to themselves. Sometimes they turned around to talk to Twink and Mary Jane, speaking just a little louder. They weren't trying to talk to me. They must have known.

The thing was, it was all my own fault. Ellie hadn't wanted me to visit Twink. Not yet, at least. But last Christmas, when I was home for vacation and feeling pretty big as a junior, I had insisted on it. It was something *I* wanted to do. Not for her, Ellie's sake. Not for Twink's. But for my own.

As we drove through the Missouri countryside, I remembered saying that. I sat trying to figure out what the hell I had meant by it. Whatever the idea was, it had been lost.

But it *wasn't* my fault, not really. I had planned the day. It was all pictured in my mind.

Father and Ellie would meet me. We would drive out to the Hill. Ellie would have plenty of time to tell me about

Twink. She would have time to tell me what to expect. How Twink would look. What the Hill was like. How many other kids there were. How to behave. Brief me, in other words, so that I wouldn't be shocked or surprised or upset.

That's the way it should have been.

The hot air coming in through the car windows seemed a little cooler finally. I put my arm across the back of the front seat, trying to look casual and under control. The gesture helped. I did feel a little better. I wondered if it would blow my father's mind to have me light a cigarette. I decided against it. It was O.K. at school, where he wouldn't see. But ever since my mother died, you just sort of knew his patience wouldn't stretch that far.

And then I changed my mind. Nuts—so what if your sixteen-year-old son has a drag once in a while? Under stress conditions, who could complain?

I lit a cigarette, trying to look cool. No one said anything. It was the longest drive of my life.

My father must have known I felt a little stronger then, because he began asking me questions about spring term. Nothing really significant. Just questions to show he was interested in what was going on. Pretty soon, Ellie joined in.

You can't very well face one direction when you're being spoken to from another. So I had to turn around. They must have counted on this for Ellie gave me a big smile, to encourage me, I guess, to take my time.

We drove a while, the three of us talking and the two girls sitting in back listening. From time to time I couldn't help sneaking fast looks at the wheelchairs, or keep myself from glancing quickly at the people in them.

Mary Jane sat thin and pale and strapped in, with her head hanging forward onto her chest. Her chin swung ever-so-slowly from right to left and back again, as though the weight of holding her head up was more than she had strength for. As though she had a terrific headache. She would look up from under her brows every once in a while at the road or at Beau or at nothing in particular. Once, her head rolled to her right shoulder. She was drooling.

Weakly, I lit another cigarette.

I recover pretty fast for a beginner. A few seconds later I was facing the back again, talking with Ellie and Father, and beginning to size up Twink.

She sat taller in her chair than Mary Jane did in hers, and she was terribly thin. She looked about as big as a skinny twelve-year-old, even though she was a few months older than me. I figured she looked so young because there were things she couldn't do for herself to keep herself in shape. Like brushing her teeth, or getting enough exercise, or eating a lot of stuff between meals.

Her legs were cased in leather braces of some kind, strapped against the leg-rests of her wheelchair. Her right arm moved in the air at her side without any direction. It wasn't a jerky movement or sudden or anything. The arm just stayed up in the air, bent at the elbow, fingers gnarled into an unusable shape. Her left arm lay quietly against the arm-rest of her chair, and her head rested on her right shoulder, a little forward.

She had gorgeous big blue eyes that seemed to be looking out at the countryside as we drove, and her mouth was open in a kind of smile. She had a nice expression, really. Maybe that sounds dumb but that's the way it struck me. A nice expression, warm and somehow sort of cheerful. And she didn't drool.

I reminded myself that now, when people asked how many kids there were in our family, I would have to say five: two boys and three girls. Sometimes I forgot. That was because, until now, I hadn't met the fifth. Ellie and Father had been married only eight months, and none of us was really used to the whole thing yet.

It's hard sometimes not to stare. I mean, you're aware of staring and aware at the same time it's not polite but you just can't help it.

I must have been staring, but not really, because I saw when Ellie smiled, reached over to Father and took his hand.

And then I did something I hadn't even been thinking about.

"Listen," I nearly shouted, speaking more to Twink than to anyone else, "if you two sex fiends are going to hold hands right here in front of us, Twink and I will just stop the car and let you walk through the woods all the way to the Hill!"

Ellie and Father laughed and held hands even more tightly. And then, from the back of the bus came a sound, that chortle thing. I strained to see Twink. She was laughing in her own way, the chortle

13

growing louder and her mouth open wide and her head held higher than before.

I laughed a little, too, and threw away my cigarette.

# Chapter Two

Christmastree Hill is an odd sort of name. Most of the trees aren't evergreens at all, just your regular, normal Midwestern kind of tree: oak, elm, cottonwood. But there are two symmetrical firs flanking the front door of the main house, an old, Victorian-looking pile of cool, brownish-red stone.

The house is old-fashioned inside, too. Parlors and solariums and two kitchens; heavy worn carpets and cut-glass lampshades and a lot of fake antique stuff on every table, shelf, and mantelpiece.

But it *feels* nice. I mean, it has a comfortable, home kind of feel about it, as though it was the kind of house you remember your grandparents having. The kind where the dining room really is big enough to have a true family dinner—without card tables being set up in the living room or in the library for the children.

And there is a hill at Christmastree Hill. It rises maybe fifty feet taller than the house below, and covers sixty acres. You get the feeling there is a lot of room to play in, to run around in and explore. Which is pretty ironic, considering.

When we pulled up to the house, there was no one in view. Beau opened the rear doors of the Volks and rolled Twink and Mary Jane out of the car. He went about this quietly and with confidence, taking care not to jar them or to surprise them by any sudden movements. He was very strong, and must have been used to lifting children in and out of wheelchairs, cars, buildings, doctors' offices.

Father stayed with Twink and Mary Jane while Ellie took me inside the house to meet Virginia, the wife of the doctor in charge of the hospital. Virginia, I gathered, was Ed's chief-assistant-in-charge-of-everything.

Virginia was easy to meet. Huge, with curly brown-gray hair and a burly voice, she shook my hand firmly as she apologized to Ellie for being in town shopping when Twink had been picked up. Then she leapt directly into all that had happened to Twink since Ellie's last visit.

After a minute of standing there with a dumb smile on my face, I began to feel a little out of place. I turned around, ready to go back outside to be with Father. My route was blocked by someone in a wheelchair. I started.

"Huh!" the voice said, pulling the chair to a stop directly in front of me.

I tried to smile. "Hi," I said, thinking it important to act as though I frequently found myself among handicapped people. I looked down into the wheelchair and saw a boy-man. I couldn't tell. Remembering how young Twink looked in comparison to her real age confused me.

"Huh," he said again. "I ... Ca-Carl ..."

"Oh," I said. "I'm Harry Walsh."

"Twinnnn-kle?" Carl managed.

"Yes, that's right," I said, sounding relieved. "I'm Twink's new brother. One of them."

"Ohhhh," Carl said, nodding wisely.

"Come on, Carl," Beau said, walking into the house. "It's too nice a day to sit inside and gossip." He wheeled Carl around very fast and eased his wheelchair down six or seven steps onto a cement veranda where Father was with the two girls. "You're going to have a picnic," Beau explained.

I followed them into the sunshine. The veranda looked out on green and yellow fields, and there was a river in the distance hiding behind a row of very dark, thick trees. I remembered a scene from a movie where there was just such a terrace in a Swiss hospital, covered with wheelchairs and patients sitting facing the sun.

Father was talking to Twink and Mary Jane, holding Twink's hand very carefully in his own. Mary Jane sat as before, but now with a big board on her lap that had been attached somehow to her wheelchair.

*"You wish that——"* my father said. "All right. Go on. *You wish that . . .* oops! You're going too fast for me, Mary Jane!"

Mary Jane's right hand was swinging over the board rapidly, dropping down to touch some part of it and then flashing upward to search again for something else.

I walked closer. The board had phrases written on it. "I want to . . . I wish that I had . . . I wish that . . . Could you get me a . . . I need to . . . sleepy now . . . ice-cream cone . . . I could read . . . milkshake . . . go to the bathroom."

"*You wish that . . . you had a*— Yes, go on," Father said happily. "Go on, I'm with you."

"I wun to the ttt . . . op a the umpie stay billing," Carl said suddenly, interrupting triumphantly.

"Really, Carl? When was that?" Ellie said, coming down into the sunlight with a tray of salad in her hands. "Carl's been to the top of the Empire State Building," she explained to me.

I nodded and tried to smile. I hadn't gotten that message at all.

"Fi . . . fi-yers . . . whun I wa in the Naaavy," Carl answered.

*The Navy!* I thought. *That must mean* . . . but Ellie shoved the tray of greens into my hands then. "You take this over there, under those trees. I'll bring Twink."

Father, Ellie, and Virginia wheeled the three kids (*kids?* I thought) over to a picnic table as I walked ahead. If Carl had been in the Navy, he couldn't have been born this way. That meant that almost anyone, *anyone* could come down with it. Anytime. Talk about mind-blowing!

As the picnic was being arranged, I looked again at Carl. I couldn't honestly

18

tell anything. He looked older than Twink but not that much. You could see he needed to shave, and that he was taller than Twink, too. But you couldn't have guessed his age. How he must hate this, I thought, after being O.K. for so many years.

Virginia swung into action then—loud, fast, and efficiently. She loaded plates with coleslaw, salad, and cold fried chicken, passing them around. Ellie took a second plate with her own over to where Twink sat beneath a tree. Virginia rolled Mary Jane over to her end of the picnic bench and placed her so she could be easily fed.

Brushing flies away from the food, feeding herself and feeding Mary Jane at the same time, Virginia began talking to me. She rattled on about how going away to school must seem, the excitement of traveling hundreds of miles each way, how grateful I must be to be able to go back East to "a really good school." I nodded a lot, which I'm pretty good at. What I mostly did was try not to watch her feed Mary Jane.

But I had nothing else to look at. I decided I wasn't that hungry. I didn't want to watch Virginia in action. My father was under a distant tree talking to Carl, and

Ellie was still with Twink. "What's that?" I finally asked Virginia, pointing to a soup-y-like white batch of stuff in a big bowl.

"Why, that's Twink's favorite food!" she laughed. "Ice cream! And, see, we've got blueberries, too!"

Her hand was quicker than my eye. From nowhere rained two buckets of blue-berries into the ice cream. Virginia stirred them together and the mixture became a horrible weakly purple color. I lit a ciga-rette.

Ellie came back from Twink's tree and scooped some ice cream and berries into a small bowl. "Why don't you come talk with us?" she said.

I followed her back to Twink's chair and sat down on the grass. There was a little breeze stirring and it was cooler there than it had been in the sun with Virginia. I felt better.

"Uhhhhh," Twink said, raising her head a little.

"Yes, dear," Ellie said. "Harry's sitting right here."

"Uhhhhh!" Twink said again.

Ellie, who had been sitting down for a moment herself, stood up. "You want to say something to Harry? Is that right?"

"Uhhhhh," Twink answered excitedly.

20

Her left hand shot out from the chair and moved restlessly.

"All right, honey," Ellie said. "Let's see. Is it a question?"

Twink's head jerked to the left, almost in answer. I watched.

"All right, a question. Does it begin with you?"

Twink made no move. Her mouth was open wide and her face pointed in Ellie's direction, waiting it seemed until the right phrase or word would be uttered.

"No, huh," Ellie said thoughtfully. "All right. Does it begin with a question? How? Why? Who——?"

But Twink's head had jerked again, in the same direction as before.

"It does!" Ellie said, smiling. "Good. Which one? How?"

Up went Twink's jaw.

"*How,*" said Ellie, thinking. "*How . . .* do you?"

No reaction.

"*How* is the . . . *How* can you . . . *How* was the——?"

That was it. Twink's head went even higher. "Uhhhh!" she said.

"Good, darling," said Ellie. "Now, let's see *How was the*——"

Twink made no sound. I couldn't explain how I knew it was "no," but I could tell.

*"How was* your——?" questioned Ellie. She was right this time. *"How was your—* Oh dear, we'll have to spell. First half of the alphabet?"

Twink made another "no" sound. "Second half?" Ellie asked. Right. "All right, now. Let's see. M? N? O? P? Q? R?"

"Uhhhh!" Twink nearly shouted.

"I passed it?" Ellie asked. "Oh my. M? N? O? P? P? All right, *P. How was your p——.* First half? Second half? First half. A, B, C, D, E, F, G, H, I, J, K, L? L? PL?* Wonderful. *How was your pl——.* All right. Here we go. First half? First half. A, B, C, D ... passed it? A? It is? Good! We're nearly there, then."

I stared. Plain staring, the kind with open mouth and bulging eyes and held-in breath.

*"How was your pla——,"* Ellie repeated, motioning for me to hand her my cigarette. She inhaled a moment and then handed it back, careful to see if Father was watching or not. "All right, Twinkle, let's go. *Pla——.* First half? Second half? First half. A, B, C, D, E, F, G ... passed it? No, not yet. O.K. H, I, J, K, L? H? I? I? Good

girl! Now we have, *How was your plai—*. Are you sure, Twink? *P, L, A, I?*"

But suddenly I knew exactly what Twink was saying. I couldt help shouting it out. "How was my plane ride?"

Twink's head shot up, nearly off the end of her neck. Her mouth broadened into what *had* to be a smile, and she laughed her own, chortling kind of laugh. Her arms circled the air and she rocked back into the wheelchair.

"How was Harry's plane ride?" Ellie asked.

"It was fine," I said, mentally elbowing Ellie out of the picture altogether. It really wasn't so hard after all. It was only a question of learning. "It was fine," I said again. "We had some really rotten food, but I was able to convince a stewardess I was old enough to have a drink, so I didn't mind the food at all."

Twink was rocking back and forth in her chair, her face still turned toward Ellie, smiling and humming, sort of, to herself. Then, suddenly, she began to agitate. Her arms became wilder and her head was lifted up again.

"Something else, darling?" Ellie asked. That was correct. "A question again?" Right, again. "How? When? Why?

Where? Why? All right, we're doing better now with Harry here to help. *Why am——? Are? Don't? Can't? Do?*"

"Can't," I said. "I think it's can't. Why can't——? Twink?"

I was right.

*"Why can't——"* Ellie said. *"Why can't you? We? They?* Oh dear. Do we have to spell again?"

Yes, said Twink, we have to spell.

"First half of the alphabet?" I asked. Nope. "Second half. O.K. M? N? O? P? Q? P? P? *Why can't p——.* First half? Right. A, B, C, D, E, F, G? I passed it? Damn! All right. I'll go more slowly. A? B? C? D? E? E? Good. *Why can't pe——.* Why can't people——?" I asked quickly. "Is that it? *Why can't people——?*"

Twink chortled happily. I was on the right track again. I can't really tell you what I felt like then. Just something a little terrific. *"Why can't people——"* I said again, squeezing.

"First half?" Ellie asked. "A? B? C? D? E? F? G? H? G? *Why can't people g——.* First half? Second half? First half. A? B? C? D? E? F? G? H? I? J? K? I passed it. All right, dear. J? I? I? *Why can't people gi——. Why can't people give ——?"*

24

Up went Twink's head and out went her arms.

*Why can't people give*——?" Ellie mused.

"You?" I asked. "You? Them? Us? Us? Great! *Why can't people give us*——. Give us what, I wonder."

Twink was almost giggling by then, in her own way. I began to think she liked my being puzzled, since *she* certainly knew all the answers to this game!

"First half?" said Ellie. "Second half. O.K., now, Twinkle. M? N? O? P? Q? R? S? T? U? V? U? T? Good, T. Now, again. First half? First half. A? B? C? D? E? F? G? H? I? J? K? L? Passed it again? All right, I'm working backward again," Ellie said. "L? K? J? I? I? *Ti*——. *Why can't people give us ti*——. Are you sure, honey? *Ti*——? Are you sure it's not T-H-E—*Why can't people give us the*——? No? O.K."

We were both stopped for a minute. Twink was in heaven, rocking back and forth, chortling away.

"T, i," I said. "Ti?"

"First half, second half," Ellie went on determinedly. "Second half. All right. M? N? N? O? Passed it *already?* Nuts! O? N? M? M. *Tim*—. Are you certain, sweetheart? Absolutely certain?"

Twink was totally, absolutely, deliciously certain.

"First half, second half?" I asked. "First half. O.K. Here goes. A? B? C? D? E? F? G? G? G? F? E? D? E? E. *Why can't people give us t-i-m-e—time! Why can't people give us time?*"

Twink relaxed. Her body sank back down into her chair and her arms quieted. She still held her head high.

*Why can't people give us time?* How could she ask a serious question like that when she was smiling?

# Chapter Three

"Headache better, dear?" Ellie asked me as I ducked into the back seat of the car, ready to leave the Hill.

I nodded. It wasn't that I was feeling better. What it was, happily, was that I wasn't feeling any worse. Because, ever since my mother died, when I stay with

Ellie and Father I catch cold. Like clockwork. I arrive home healthy. Within two or three days bang!—my nose runs, my eyes water, my temperature rises, and I spend the rest of the two weeks pampering myself and feeling stupid.

And it *is* stupid. We had all been prepared for Mother's death. We had all known it was going to happen, even Mother. The night before her funeral I'd had a great sleep. But when I woke up and dressed the next day, I looked and felt as though that day were going to be my last. And it nearly was, with the people and the flowers and the cars and all.

Psychosomatic maybe, but the piles of Kleenex next to the bed are very real.

This time, though, I was thinking ahead. I'd been taking cold pills already for five days. Nothing but nothing was going to put me off my schedule this time. Which was why Ellie asked how I was feeling. I had just excused myself to take a couple of "aspirin" for a "headache."

We pulled away from the Hill in late afternoon, tired. We'd finished all the purple delight Virginia had on hand, and had spent the day "talking" with Twink, Mary Jane, and Carl.

Carl had this thing about interrupting.

It drove you a little nuts. But he was always so pleased at being able to get something out and to have it understood that you couldn't really be angry. Besides, the day was a special one for him. Here were three people with whom he could remember life as it had been before he'd come to the Hill. He was on Cloud Nine. I was below the horizon. It was depressing.

Mary Jane's questions and answers weren't connected very well. Her thoughts seemed to come fast and to disappear just as fast. She couldn't keep her mind on anything for more than a few seconds. Her arm flew up and down her word-board. By the time you understood what it was she was saying and were ready to answer in return, she was hard at work on another thought, a different question. Ellie said this was because her mind was so fast and her arm so much slower. It seemed to me that both were setting all-time speed records. After a while it was almost funny. Almost.

Twink's questions had to do with her new family. With me and Bobby and Jane. I tried very hard to be objective so that she wouldn't be too much prejudiced. Bobby, for example, is supposed to be some sort of weird mechanical genius. I think he's just a smart-ass. And no one really knows much about Jane so far. She's only seven.

But Twink wanted to know everything. What we looked like, what we liked doing best. Did we like music? Did we go to movies and watch television a lot? Had we met Whizzer? (Had we? Wow!) Were we any good at sports? Things like this that after a while bugged me because I would have thought Ellie had filled her in a little.

Still, it was sensational being able to understand Twink, helping Father and Ellie work out some of her thoughts faster than they would have done alone. I began to think that maybe they were too close to Twink and needed someone like me around, someone with a little perspective, a sort of freshness, to get things really moving.

So when the gnats that had been buzzing around the Hill during lunch turned into cocktail-time mosquitoes, we said good-bye to Twink, piled into Ellie's car, and headed for the freeway, Chicago, and home. The yellow and green of the fields had become gray and dark blue. The locusts had been rubbing their legs together for nearly an hour. Swifts soared and dove above the trees along the river.

We drove for about twenty minutes

with no one speaking, looking forward, I guess, to getting home and remembering things we all had to do when we got there. I was trying to figure out why Valerie Bock had stopped writing, and if it meant anything special, when my mouth opened and out came the first of seven hundred questions I'd collected at the Hill.

"Then it's not always brain damage at birth, is it?" I asked.

"What?" Father said.

"Well, look at Carl! Obviously, he wasn't that way when he was born."

Ellie turned around to explain. "Accidents in adult life sometimes result in brain damage. That's cerebral palsy, too."

"But isn't there any kind of cure? Any strengthening, or anything?"

"Some people think it's possible to retrain different parts of the brain to handle the jobs the damaged part should do," Ellie answered. "And sometimes this can be successful, in a small way." Then she laughed. "You wouldn't believe some of the theories John and I used to run into after Twink was born."

"Like what? I asked, as the very tall figure in a photograph of Twink's father flicked across my mind.

"Well, I remember one mother telling

me—years ago, at an American Medical Association meeting, I think—that a good case of smallpox could restore damaged brain cells. Can you imagine? And she was deadly serious!"

"Can it?"

"I don't really know, Harry," Ellie said. "But no one in his right mind is going to try to find out."

"How did you find out about Twink?" I asked. "I remember a movie once where this kid was deaf and dumb and no one knew about it for months. The only way they figured it out was when the kid wouldn't cry or react to anything that happened. How did you know?"

"Simple. The day after she was born, the doctor told us."

I had a sudden thought. Maybe Ellie would rather not remember all this. And then I had another one: she's a tough lady. She can tell me to buzz off if she wants. Or Father can.

"There was nothing melodramatic about it," Ellie said. "There wasn't time to picture Twink growing up healthy and going to college and getting married and the usual things parents think about when they have children—the things John and I had thought about earlier when

31

Whizzer came along. There wasn't even time, at first, to feel sorry for ourselves. We had no real idea what cerebral palsy meant. We had to learn."

"What about your families?" I asked. "How did they take it?"

"Oh, one or two people got upset and stopped calling or visiting. But everyone else did what they could to help out. And we need all the help we could get."

For some funny reason, I thought about my Aunt Gail. There was always a contest between her and my mother. Whatever Mother got, Gail had to have, but bigger. If my mother was given a silver tea service or something like that for an anniversary or a birthday, the next day Gail was out scouring the town for a bigger, better, glossier set. What floated into my mind then was Gail trying to beat this trick. It would have driven her crazy!

"Are you sure you want to hear all this?" Ellie asked me suddenly. "I mean, some of it isn't very pretty."

So much for that sudden thought I had. "Well, at least I won't be surprised by anything any more," I said. "Besides, Twink is part of the family. I know about *our* part of the family, and some of *that* is pretty wild."

"No unbiased reports with Harry," my father said.

"None for me, either," Ellie answered. "Give me one of your cigarettes, Harry."

"Eleanor," Father said.

"Oh, Kenneth," Ellie sighed. "I don't have any matches. I just want to play with it."

"When *you* gave up smoking," I reminded Father, "I remember coming into the bathroom one morning and finding you sneaking a puff in the shower."

Ellie laughed.

Just then it began to rain. Damn! I thought, watching dead bugs being flooded off the windshield, fishing around in my pockets for another cold pill. I tried swallowing it cold, and ended up chewing it instead. It was not the most exciting new taste sensation.

I began thinking of questions about Twink I wanted answered. Like when she first realized she was different from other kids, and what about being a girl and being different? And what about Twink's accident?

By the time I realized Ellie had begun her story, I'd missed some of it. But that was mostly stuff I could catch up with later. I tuned in.

# Chapter Four

The thing was (I remember Ellie saying) that when Twink was little she looked like any other little kid. She had big blue eyes and she gurgled and made regular baby-type sounds, and her hair grew and her teeth came in and everything seemed pretty standard.

But Ellie and John, knowing from the beginning what was coming, had been in action for months.

Right after the doctor's announcement, John headed for the hospital's medical library. He came back nearly empty-handed: two books and a dictionary definition—"a disability resulting from damage to the brain before or during birth and outwardly manifested by muscular incoordination and speech disturbances."

The first book was called *The Little Locksmith*. It was about the trials of a hunchbacked little girl. Though it was ridiculous and old-fashioned, John read it aloud to Ellie in the hospital. They were younger then, and they laughed at the melodrama. But not very loudly.

The second book was more useful. It was by a guy who had cerebral palsy and had made good in spite of it. *A Wayward Stork* was the story of a man named Parker who grew up at home, went to public schools, worked his way through med school and ended up founding his own home for C.P. kids. The book was ten years old even then, but it held special information that Ellie and John felt would be helpful in the future.

As soon as she was strong enough, Ellie went to work in a day-care center for crippled children. Twink stayed at home with Whizzer and a nurse who came in each day.

Ellie got right in the middle of it all. She fed, washed, dressed, played with, taught those kids about life—their kind and ours. She knew she had to learn as much as she could as fast as she could, for Twink wouldn't always be just another cute little bundle in diapers.

And though John joined every group that had anything to do with cerebral palsy and attended as many medical conventions and meetings as he could, he soon realized that the amount of solid information available was pretty small. He and Ellie would have to figure things out for themselves as they went along.

As soon as Ellie felt she had learned the basic skills needed, she dismissed the day nurse and took care of Twink by herself. She did the things any mother would for any normal baby.

It was months before Twink's differences began to show. She grew and gurgled and giggled and slept and ate and was a baby, plain and simple. She learned to focus on things and to reach out in their direction. She played with her toys, bumping them around her crib and pushing them through its slats onto the floor.

Pretty soon Twink was even moving around. But on her back. It must have been weird to see, this pink little kid scrambling across a floor as though she were sneaking under barbed wire beneath a river of tracer bullets.

Twink's first big difficulty (besides sitting unsupported) was crawling on all fours. She hadn't the control to pull her legs up when she wanted, or to keep her hands down on the floor to support herself. Her limbs weren't dependable and her back wasn't strong.

But her head had no weaknesses. She was a whiz. If she couldn't do something one way, she did it another. So there she would be, flat on her back, her tiny arms circling overhead as her legs contracted and relaxed, pushing her along the carpet. And she was fast! If there hadn't already been one child nick-named Whizzer in the family, Twink would have been the one.

The only problem, Ellie told me, was that Twink couldn't see where she was going most of the time. She was apt to bump into things suddenly and hurt her head. So all the legs of the furniture in Ellie and John's apartment were covered in thick, soft carpet. Shock absorbers.

Ellie began thinking about sending Twink to the day-care center. From people more qualified than she felt herself to be, Ellie knew Twink could get speech training and proper exercise. At home, she and John could work with Twink on basic things like counting and, later, spelling and reading.

In his book, Parker had insisted that a C.P. might look funny on the outside but on the inside be absolutely fantastic. The learning part of a child's brain was often unaffected by damage to its other parts. Coping with life was to be a part of it, and the best therapy available as a child grew ready for it would be a normal school life, if possible.

And that was what Ellie and John hoped for at the beginning. That with good therapy and real school training, Twink might learn to walk, to talk, and even be able to go to a local high school. That as she got older, her nervous center could be rearranged somehow, redirected, so that the sudden movements she couldn't control as a child *could* be controlled as she grew older by improving her concentration. That was what Dr. Parker had been able to do. That was the hope for Twink.

I remembered driving to California last summer with Ernie and Peter Dugan. One morning we stopped for breakfast at the main hotel in Cheyenne, Wyoming. Ernie went into the dining room to get a table while Peter and I looked around the lobby. There were a dozen huge tanks filled with water, seaweed, sand, and tropical fish of all kinds and colors.

On one tank there was a small cardboard sign: "See the Rare, Invisible Indonesian Fighting Fish!" The tank was all lit up and the water plants swayed gently as though pushed by faint currents or a fish.

Peter had stood beside the tank staring for nearly five minutes.

# Chapter Five

"But if you felt that way," I said, "why did you send Twink away so soon? I mean, you could have kept her home until she *was* ready for school."

"There was one reason we couldn't," Ellie said. "You'd never guess it, not in a million years."

"What?" I asked. "The strain on you?"

"No," Ellie smiled. "The reasons's even simpler. We—John and I—might have kept Twink from growing. We, who cared more than anyone and wanted her to get so strong."

"I don't understand."

"We would have been too helpful." Ellie said. "For example, by holding Twink's shoulders as she tried to learn to walk, by bracing her from behind, she would come to depend on us too much. She wouldn't try her hardest. She'd know we were always standing by to stop her from falling."

Ellie punched a button on the dashboard and leaned back. "It was," she said, "the hardest lesson I ever had to learn."

She pulled the lighter from its place near an ashtray and lit the cigarette she'd held for the past half hour. Father frowned but said nothing.

"I take that back," she said then. "It wasn't the hardest lesson. It was only the first of the hardest lessons I ever learned."

While Twink was a whiz at crawling (Ellie had continued), zigzagging happily across the floor until a malignant table leg or door zapped her, she wasn't so hot at walking. Her back wasn't strong enough to keep her upright, and although she could be held up, supported by Ellie or John, her feet wouldn't rest flatly on the floor.

Seeing her held up, dangling, one saw that her feet never relaxed. Her toes crinkled and unfolded, and the soles of her feet were turned inward, heels held high in spite of themselves. "Muscular inversion" it was called.

So Twink got her first set of braces. She was still too young at a year and a half to be fitted completely. The more complicated and uncomfortable back-brace that might have allowed her to begin working at walking was still too heavy. But she could be fitted for the difficulty with her feet. She took her first supported steps at about the time Bea Donald arrived.

Bea Donald was a young woman from farm country, a bright-eyed, curly-haired happy blonde who loved kids and, miraculously, had a nurse's diploma. Being single at twenty-two, she had come to Chicago to work in a hospital, registering with the local chapter of the medical society as a private nurse, too.

By this time (Ellie said) she and John had discovered that while they *could* handle things as they happened, they weren't at all certain their solutions were the *best* ones. They were nervous. For while Twink was a sunny kind of kid, she was also strong. Simple things, like dressing and feeding, were becoming difficult.

Not that Twink consciously fought. But if and when she did, she couldn't help it.

She just couldn't control her limbs. Bathtime became an amphibious assault, part of the struggle happening above the waterline, and part of it sometimes taking place beneath the waves.

Ellie felt she needed help. Bea wanted to give it. So while Bea made arrangements to move into the apartment, Twink was taken out to the Annandale Clinic for a complete examination and an up-to-the-minute diagnosis.

But for a famous place that was supposed to be able to perform all sorts of fantastic miracles regardless of the disease, the doctors there seemed to know less than Ellie and John about brain-damaged children. They seemed to know little about the causes, and even less about the possible treatment of cerebral palsy. They refused to advise. They wouldn't give hope.

One doctor did mention, finally, the only man who might be able to give Ellie and John whatever help really was available: Dr. Parker, the guy who had grown up successfully with all of his handicaps. John wrote to Parker in New York City and made an appointment. They left Twink and Whizzer with Bea, a bit nervously since they felt they didn't really know her well yet, and flew East.

42

The appointment had been made for just after lunch. John and Ellie arrived early and sat in the doctor's outer office, waiting. A few minutes after two, a gnome-like man appeared and made his way, on braces and aluminum crutches, through the office.

"I . . . am . . . sorry . . . to . . . beee . . . laaay," he said huskily. "I'll beee wi . . . you . . . in a mo-mo-ment."

In a gray oatmeal tweed suit that looked seven sizes too big, the man struggled on toward his office door. He had a lumbering, rolling kind of walk, hoisting himself along from one foot to the other, shorter foot.

Ellie and John, still, watched. The man threw his crutches forward, seemed to hunch himself together from inside for the effort, and then lifted his entire body and heaved it forward. Powerful, outsized shoulders held the weight in midair until he landed and then thrust his crutches forward again.

Ellie looked across the room at the receptionist, questioning her with open mouth and wide eyes. The woman smiled a "yes." Ellie stood quickly and burst toward the door of the office, already running as she reached the long hall outside.

John caught up with her as she stood waiting for an elevator. She was crying.

"I didn't know!" she said. "It's so terrible! So unfair!"

"But we *don't* know," John said. "We don't know *anything* yet."

"Just think," Ellie gasped, "that's Parker! That's the man who worked and fought and ... *that's* what he became! Twink'll be like that. Twink may not be able to do so well!"

"We don't know what Twink will be able to do when she gets older," John said. "She may be even luckier."

"Luckier!" Ellie shouted, almost laughing through her tears.

*"He* thinks he's lucky," John said. "You can't take that away from him."

"No. You ca-can't," Dr. Parker said, hoisting himself around a corner.

Ellie jumped and spun around at the same time. John put his arm around her. They waited.

"For ... whom ... are ... you ... feeling," he said. Then he added. "Sorry?"

Ellie stared at him. He was smiling. The question was interested and concerned, not angry or accusing. "I don't know," she admitted. "I don't know."

"Let us ... ta-talk about ... it," Dr.

Parker suggested, throwing his body back around to walk to his office. Ellie and John followed.

They learned that afternoon to adjust to Parker's voice. They learned to wait, patiently, for him to finish saying what he wanted to without interrupting and finishing his statements for him. They learned about his school in Florida, and a little about his wife, his friends, his life. They learned to like and to trust him. And they learned they would have to give up Twink.

"Because," Parker said with effort, "because even *she* deserves her own life. A life apart from your problems and your sympathy." He smiled to himself. "And so, to be truthful, do you. Deserve a life apart from your worries about her. You are so young yet. You have another, perfect child."

"But Twink's only two," Ellie said. "Surely that's too early to start trying to teach her things."

"It isn't," Parker said. "Whatever your hopes are for her, they take time. And it takes strength and teaching to make even the slimmest hope honest. There is one more thing," he added. "Some days she will be bright and beautiful. You will

45

think great progress can be made, will be made, tomorrow. But tomorrow comes and the brightness has gone. The hope will have gone, too. It takes time and strength and teaching even to keep hoping."

Uneasy, but believing in Parker, Ellie and John agreed. They would bring Twink to school at the end of the month. They would even try to persuade Bea to go with her, to live there and care for her there. Dr. Parker was delighted at the thought of an extra, strong and trained hand. And Ellie and John were free, as were all parents, to visit as often as they liked—after school hours.

As soon as the taxi pulled away from Parker's building in New York, Ellie began to doubt. Were they doing what was best for Twink? Best for themselves and Whizzer? "I'm a very strong person," she told John. "I can handle Twink. I could teach her. I could even go back to school and learn about therapy and speech training. Why couldn't I do it all?"

John said nothing. There was nothing to say. He knew, and Ellie knew, and Dr. Parker had known all along.

At the end of their journey, when they reached their own apartment, Bea didn't answer their calls. She seemed to be hiding somewhere. But rocketing out to greet Ellie and John, riding in her own fashion the original skate-board, was a fuzzy pink bundle in head-to-toe snuggies. Ellie felt the impact just below her knee as she heard Whizzer giggle behind the door.

For Bea had welded a small plastic-mold modern wraparound chair onto a short but strong piece of walnut, slanting the chair in such a way that Twink seemed to be sitting up nearly straight. Attached to the back of the chair and extending into space was a crash-panel, also made of walnut and covered by pieces of an old quilt. This now hit stationary obstacles where before Twink's head would have. She was still motoring backward, to be sure, but now with speed and comparative safety.

Ellie said that after having decided to give Twink up to Dr. Parker, what she and John really didn't need at home was a rosy-cheeked, clean, and happy-sounding kid with bows above her ears holding back her light brown curls. Instantly their new determination began to waver. But within days, Ellie and John and Bea realized that teaching Twink anything at home was nearly impossible.

An odd routine was beginning to be established. Days began with breakfast. After the kitchen and Twink's high chair had been cleaned and repaired, Twink was ready for bathing and dressing. She was set for her lessons by lunchtime. But by then it *was* lunchtime. After the floors and walls had been wiped down, Twink needed to be straightened up. By mid-afternoon, finally ready to learn, she was fit only for napping. Dinner was another battle, and by the time it was finished, everyone was too tired to clean either the kitchen or Twink—and she was put to bed. Whizzer began to learn what "fending for oneself" meant.

There were moments of fun, Ellie remembered. There were times when she and John, or Bea and herself, would feel real teaching progress was being made. But the awareness of each meal's effort almost made them overlook these altogether. Every day's first thought was last night's memory; each morning's second thought was of that night's certain exhaustion.

It wasn't Twink's fault, any of this. She certainly didn't mean to kick a table leg and shake over a pitcher of milk. She couldn't help it. Nor could she stop the sweep of a runaway arm across her high chair's tray, cascading its contents onto the linoleum below.

And while a few scrapes and scratches earned in the line of duty dressing or bathing or feeding Twink bothered no one, as she grew older, Twink would grow stronger.

# Chapter 6

After the long black-and-white ride on the train from Chicago, arriving in Florida seemed like walking from the street into a brilliant technicolor movie. Ellie and John and Bea felt they could hardly see: everything seemed newly washed, freshly painted, and carefully shined.

As the taxicab turned off the main road and headed toward Parker's, Ellie strained to see through the trees for a first view of Twink's new home-to-be. Everything remained hidden until the car rounded the last turn on the gravel.

"Oh, Twink!" cried Bea. "See how beautiful it is! Ohhh, it's just beautiful!"

The taxi driver laughed at Bea's surprise and spoke into his rear-view mirror. "And she'll have some mighty interesting people here, as friends." He laughed again to himself. "I remember the '48 hurricane. We sure had some time then. The whole town got to know them kids. And like 'em."

Something in the man's voice was reassuring to John, and he said so as he paid him. "Don't you worry," the driver said. "Why, these kids are like our own. There are some funny ones among 'em, but mostly they're just like neighbor kids."

Bea took Twink in her arms and walked around to the front of the old house, which stood looking out at the sea. Ellie made it sound like someone's dream of what Spain should be, in Florida, in the 1920's. Two stories high, stucco and whitewashed brick and red-tile roofs. The only major change Parker had made in "Lago del Mar" when he bought it was in its grounds. The grass was longer and less well-cared for, so that tumbling kids landed just a little more softly.

"Welcome!" called a tiny, quick-moving woman as she came down the steps to shake hands. "I'm Gretel Parker," she announced with a smile.

"Come," she said to Ellie and John in her German accent. "I'll show you around as your daughter is settled." She waved at two men standing in some distant shade. They came at her beckoning, but slowly and with effort.

C.P.'s.

Ellie hesitated. Where was Twink going? Who would help Bea? "Be easy," said Mrs. Parker. "Here we all help. Come," and she took Ellie's hand.

She spoke quickly and quietly as she led Ellie and John into the main house, through its long bright halls, into large meeting rooms, through a library and a game room, a common room for private visits, the kitchen and the enormous dining room. "There are more than one hundred of us," Mrs. Parker said.

Upstairs were quarters for the staff in one wing and, in another, single and double rooms for children over twelve. The furniture was cheery and simple. The rooms were clean. Not necessarily neat—"Children," Mrs. Parker shrugged with a smile—but clean, comfortable and homey. "We *are* home, you see," she said happily, "to all our children."

The house was flooded with light. The rooms were filled with signs of children who needed, among the things all children need, special "different" things: braces and grips and guide rails along walls; clothes and games and books; ramps instead of stairs; toys and flowers and trophies; crutches and wheelchairs photographs and mementos of lives left before most memories began.

Ellie and John were led out onto the playground between the main house and a white clapboard house a few hundred yards away on the beach. There were two small groups of children sunning themselves on the lawn. Others were in classes. Midmorning was a busy but quiet time, and from the long, low school building came a hum that seemed to harmonize with the tone of the calm sea beyond.

John thought the building might once have been a stable. There was a long hall dividing it, with two large rooms at either end. Several medium-size rooms blossomed off the hall in between. One of the large rooms was equipped with a film projector and a screen and had a small stage. The smaller rooms were devoted to special purposes: one for arts and crafts, one for reading, one for arithmetic, two for physical therapy—exercises that children did under general, easy supervision, and exercises that required special equipment and the help of trained personnel.

Ellie and John peeked quickly into each room. They stood listening to a class; they saw children in water therapy; they watched the staff in action. And then they came to the last room in the building, the large room at the other end of the hall. The nursery.

Mrs. Parker swung open double doors and Ellie and John walked into a dormitory-type room with cribs and small beds and baby-size furniture. This was where the youngest children lived. There was only one child in the room then: Twink.

Ellie rushed forward. She had seen children struggling with yarn and sewing cards. She had seen children in whirlpool baths hanging on to steel rims for their very lives. She had heard the school's finest teacher, Dr. Brownlee, speak about American history and had understood nothing the man said. She had seen the staff, almost all dressed normally but few of them "normal." She had seen Twink's new companions. She had no intention of leaving her daughter here.

"Where's Bea?" Ellie asked as she picked up Twink.

"Getting settled in her room," Mrs. Parker said pleasantly. Then she reached out her arms for Twink who chortled and smiled and stretched out *her* arms for Mrs. Parker. "As soon as Bea is settled," Mrs. Parker said, taking Twink from her mother, "she and Twink will begin to explore. There will be no classes for her right away."

Ellie stood as though in shock. Mrs. Parker still held Twink who seemed perfectly happy to be held as she was carried toward the door. John and Ellie had no choice but to follow.

"I suspect Twink is a very bright little girl," Mrs. Parker said as she led them back across the playground. "She has such bright eyes. How right that she is called 'Twinkle.'"

"Mrs. Parker," Ellie began, "I really don't think we're prepared to——"

"I know she will like it here with us. We have our own world right here on the beach. Why, we have children from Sweden and from Argentina. From Rio and from Los Angeles."

"I'm sure it's lovely here. It's very nice," Ellie said. "But for Twink——"

"And it's perfect for your daughter," Mrs. Parker said quickly with a smile. She waved at a car on the drive. "When you come at Christmas, you will be surprised how well she has learned things. And your friend Bea will keep you very well informed of her progress."

A taxi stopped on the gravel a few feet from the four of them. The driver leaned over the front seat and pushed open the back door nearest Ellie.

"We have a Christmas play and everyone takes a part. And when spring comes, we climb into our train and go where it is cool," said Mrs. Parker, shaking hands with John. "We have picnics and fairs and contests and fun. But we are here first to learn!"

John leaned across his wife and closed the cab's door. Mrs. Parker took Twink's hand in hers and waved. The taxi moved forward, slowly at first but then more swiftly, and the ride to the airport was made easier by the driver who seemed somehow to know he was supposed to talk soothingly.

# Chapter Seven

At least the weather for Twink's first day at Parker's was nice, I thought, listening to Ellie. Our weather, beyond the windows of Ellie's car, was rotten. The roadside was blurred dull gray and black by our speed. We'd been driving for more than an hour and the rain hadn't stopped once. Miraculously, my sniffles had.

"There's one of those orange roofs ahead," said Father, letting the car glide into the right-hand "off" lane. "Anyone besides me want coffee?"

Ellie nodded yes. Gratefully, I thought.

I checked. No, I wasn't exactly hungry. Just a little touchy down there. It would probably be all to the good to keep up my strength.

Actually, that's another weird psychothing I have. I get hungry all the time. Not really, though. What it is, is if I have an exam, or a game, or have to go someplace I don't know anyone, I get nervous. And nervous for me means hungry. I eat all the time.

I usually put it down to the fact that I'm a growing boy, and it can't do any harm. I figure I can keep it up until I'm twenty-five or so. Then I'll probably have to cut back or have heart failure.

As we walked into one of H. Johnson's finest, I decided not to ask Ellie more questions for a while. When she'd finished about leaving Twink at the Parkers', her voice had an extra edge to it. Not sad, exactly, but not happy—as if she remembered, as she spoke, seeing Twink off on a dangerous mountain climb, a trek up a treacherous peak that should only have been looked at and thought beautiful from a distance. I guess maybe Ellie had already jumped ahead in her mind and glimpsed the accident happening.

Also, I was beginning to thing about Valerie Bock again. I remembered her last letter. She'd just been elected secretary of an all-school advisory board or something. The president, I was informed, was a guy named Bill Peck, who was captain of the basketball team and who, I was further informed (I remembered thinking even then that I didn't need to have *all* this information!), was "just fantastic looking!"

Swell.

After a "fan*tas*tic looking" plate of fried clams (frozen, I think), French fries, a vanilla shake, and coffee, I followed Father and Ellie back to the car. I had already decided that if basketball meant more to Valerie than soccer and lacrosse, that was *her* problem. I certainly wasn't going to stand in the way of her housewifely happiness.

Actually, there wasn't much point in trying to ask Ellie any more questions then. I was too angry.

Fantastic, indeed!

After a while I dozed, listening to the hiss of trucks we passed and seeing through closed eyes the lights of service areas along the roadside. But I kept having weird switches in mid-dream. There would be Twink as a Valerie-kind of girl, all leggy and pink, soft and dancing. Then I'd get a shot of Valerie wrapped in leather and wheelchair-bound, mouth open, arms swiveling, eyes distant. Two or three times I woke not knowing where I was.

Where we were, soon enough, was driving past Comisky Park. It wasn't the fastest way home, but I guess Father remembered I thought the Outer Drive the most beautiful thing in Chicago. Soon we were passing the Museum of Science and Industry, then Buckingham Fountain. The lights of the city blinked together as we passed the Hilton, whisked around the van der Rohe buildings, looped the Drake, and whizzed by the Ambassadors to home. As we piled out of the car and unloaded its trunk, I peeked quickly across the street. Old Bock the Block wasn't home. That was probably just as well. There were certainly more important things to think about and do than worry about old Heavy Hips.

I was trying to think of just *one* as I walked down the hall, lugging my suitcases, toward our front door. But there wasn't a lot of time for thinking of *any-*thing really, for as Father put his key in the lock, the door was opened from the inside and there stood Whizzer, all grubby and green and shouting "Hello, *hello!*"

# PART TWO

## Chapter One

Ellie and Kenneth kissed Whizzer hello in quick succession, Ellie with a little hug that was more tired than affectionate, Kenneth with one a bit more enthusiastic. Harry stood outside in the hall, watching.

"Well," Whizzer said, smiling, broadly but feeling shy, "this is *your* home, too, Harry. Come on in."

Harry picked up his suitcases and stepped over the threshold. Before he could stop her, or put down his bags to do the same, Whizzer embraced him lightly. Harry seemed to break down somewhat, and smiled at his stepsister.

"I mean, don't get all unraveled," Whizzer said. "We've only met once. You're not expected to do handsprings or anything."

"Hi, Whizzer," Harry said, letting his suitcases slide to the floor at his sides.

"Darling," Ellie said to Whizzer as she took off her coat. "Will you excuse me? I'm absolutely bushed. Are you staying here tonight?"

"I thought I would," Whizzer answered, kicking off her paint-splattered boots and trying to fit five-feet-ten into an antique Oriental chair. "I made up the bed in the study."

"Oh well, then I'll see you in the morning," Ellie decided. "Harry, welcome home, dear. I hope the summer is a super one for us all."

"Night, Mom," Whizzer said.

"I'll call Gail," Kenneth said, making a small drink for himself at a sideboard, "and check on Bob and Jane. I'll be in soon, sweetheart."

"Night all," Ellie said as she kicked off her shoes and disappeared down a darkened hallway.

"You kids want anything?" Kenneth offered.

"No thanks, Dad," Harry said. "Maybe later."

"You know where everything is," his father added. "I'll catch the ten o'clock news. Be in the study if you want any-thing."

"Right."

Kenneth stopped suddenly as he was nearly out of the room. He turned around and smiled a genuine smile at Whizzer. "Everything copacetic?" he asked gently.

"Super," Whizzer answered. She blew him a kiss.

Harry watched all this standing near the fireplace. Before he was really able to think about it, he was alone with Whizzer. He shuffled his feet on the hearth, then decided to take off his blazer.

"Wow!" Whizzer cried in mock ecstasy. "Alone together at last!"

Harry smiled. "Your dream come true."

"Not ex*act*ly," Whizzer said.

There was a rather long moment be-tween them. Whizzer cleared her throat. "Hey, Harry, you wanna be friends?"

Harry chuckled nervously. He lit a ciga-rette.

"I *mean* it," Whizzer said.

"Well," Harry started. "I mean, you don't have to feel obligated or anything. Just because we're related."

"I'm not kidding, Harry. I know it's sort of rough, being attacked like this by someone you hardly know. The thing is, *my* bag is honesty."

Harry held up his left hand and made a small circle of it, putting it to his eye. With his other hand, he made cranking motions forward. His camera scanned Whizzer from head to toe and back up again. "Vell," he growled as Germanicly as possible, "zer is somezing about you, somezing zat might be right for ze part of ze older voman." He paused. "You *are* a voman, yes?"

"From time to time," Whizzer said.

Harry put his camera down. "Last time I saw you, you looked more like one."

Whizzer looked down at herself. Green bell-bottoms, cable-knit green sweater, a green scarf holding her hair back from her forehead. All rumpled. "At least I'm not color-blind," she said. "There *is* a point to it all."

"What?"

"It keeps Mother from worrying."

"That doesn't make much sense," Harry said.

"Yes, it does. She nearly died when I finished Northwestern and decided to get my own place. She fussed like crazy. I couldn't afford it; I'd never furnish it properly; I certainly wouldn't be making enough money to pay the rent. She was wrong, of course. I did all that. But to put her mind at ease, so she won't think I'm living in sin or smoking grass or dropping acid or being kept by some furious Mafia-type, when I come around here I look as unappetizing as possible."

"I would think, if you wanted her not to worry, you'd look as nice as possible when you saw her."

"How worried can you get about sex when you see a big-boned Amazon-type with grease and paint under her finger-nails?"

"You mean you don't do any of those things?" Harry asked.

Whizzer smiled gently, conscious then of the six years between herself and Harry. "I said we could be friends, not confessors, Harry."

Harry blushed.

"How was your visit with Twink?" Whizzer asked.

"Pretty unnerving," Harry answered after a minute. "There's a lot I don't understand."

"Can I help?"

"Probably," said Harry, "but it would take a lot of time. I've four thousand questions."

"Like what?"

"Well, on the way back Ellie talked about it, some. She told about Twink's being a baby and all, and about her going down to Florida."

"And then?" Whizzer asked.

"Then," said Harry, lighting a cigarette, "then we had supper. I didn't see much point in asking too many things. I thought it was probably upsetting her."

"You're O.K., you know, Harry," Whizzer said softly. "Because you're right. It does upset Mother to talk about it. It wipes her out every time she visits Twink. Guilt, of course. Beyond sadness, I mean."

"Even after all this time?" Harry wondered.

"Even now," Whizzer said.

"But that nurse, Bea. Ellie said she went to Florida with Twink. Like so much furniture or extra bedding. Shipped out and sent down. Didn't she have anything to say about it?"

"Of course she did," Whizzer answered. "She wanted to go. She was thrilled. She'd never been to Florida. It was exciting for her."

Quickly Whizzer stood and started toward her former room at the rear of the apartment. "I've got old pictures, some letters and things," she said. "Started collecting them when I was eleven or twelve, I guess. I'll get them."

Before Harry could agree, she was gone. He hadn't meant to talk about this to Whizzer. In fact, not knowing she would be at home, he hadn't imagined talking to her at all. Their only previous visit had been short, polite, formal, and uneasy.

Still, Harry thought, what else did they have in common? At least now. Except Twink.

Desperately, Harry culled his brain for bits and pieces of information he'd been given about Whizzer. There wasn't much. She was twenty-two, six years older than Twink. She was handsome rather than pretty, tall and independent. Like her father, he supposed.

"What made me think of all this," Whizzer said, carrying two large bundles wrapped in ribbon into the room, "was what you said about Bea. I never really got to know her very well. By the time I might have been able to understand her a little, she had left to get married."

Whizzer sprawled on the carpet in front of the fireplace. She smiled up at Harry.

Harry smiled back. "What do you think?" she asked.

"About what?"

"Us. Think we'll make it?"

Harry grinned. "Has there ever been anyone you wanted to be friends with you weren't?"

"Once," Whizzer said. "But I've blocked out his name."

She opened the ribbon around one packet of papers. For a few seconds she thumbed through letters, snapshots, souvenirs. "Ah, she said, pulling a yellowed piece of notepaper from the pile. "Here it is."

"What?"

"The first letter Mother ever got from Bea. After she and Twink got settled in at Parker's. I found it maybe ten years later than it happened." She smiled sympathetically. "You know, I could almost recite this word for word."

"How come?"

"Because I remember when I found it. I pictured Bea as she was then—young and pretty and full of life—and then I pictured where she was."

"Read it," said Harry.

Whizzer began.

68

Dear Mrs. Munson:

Well, our first day here is over, and Twink is sound asleep. I snuck down to peek at her, and I guess she's going to settle down here easy as pie.

My room in the other building is very nice. I have a window that looks onto the ocean, and there is a nice breeze. Tomorrow I'll try to find some flowers to make it look a little homier. I'm awfully glad I brought pictures of my family with me. On my bureau, they make me feel not quite so lonely.

I hope you won't mind my saying this. But I'm a little frightened here. Not that everyone hasn't been just wonderful. Mrs. Parker is very nice, and she has gone out of her way to make me feel at home.

But still, everywhere I look I'm a sort of freak. You'd think the others would be. The sick people, I mean, who live here all the time. But that isn't so. Everyone except Mrs. Parker, one cook, and one therapist has C.P.

Some are worse than others, of course. Most of the teachers and therapy people are better off than the kids, anyway.

I guess I just feel out of place. Probably feeling sorry for myself, too. Tomorrow will be better. I think I'll go outside then and into town to look around. I'm pretty good at making friends, and people seemed real nice when we got here. You remember.

I guess that's all the news there is for now. I hope you won't be angry at me for writing all this, but I didn't know who else I could say it to. I'll take good care of Twink, I promise. And I will write very soon again. Say hello to your husband for me.

Your friend, Bea.

# Chapter Two

"But what about you?" Harry asked slowly, thinking of the loneliness in Bea's letter.

"Me?" Whizzer said, thumbing through the papers on the floor in front of her.

"Yes, I mean, being the older sister. Sort of put aside while everyone worried so about Twink."

"Oh," Whizzer chuckled quietly. "You mean 'sibling rivalry' and all that. Jealousy and envy and tantrums."

"Exactly," nodded Harry.

"Well, truthfully, for a long time I was your perfect unhappy child. I went through all that. And then, later on, I'd say when I was about ten, I finally realized what was what. I got over it all."

"And that's it?"

"That's all there is worth talking about," Whizzer said. "Most of the damage kids suffer really isn't damage at all. It's parents worrying that it *might* be."

Harry stood up and went to the sideboard. "Do you want a drink?" he asked. "I do."

"This get you down?"

"No. Not now, not here, anyway. I want to hear it all."

"There's not so much as all that," Whizzer said. "All we have is the story of a little kid, part of whose life was happy. Part of whose life was a wreck."

"Well," Harry said, turning back with his drink in hand, "I don't have to hear everything tonight. Just what *you* feel up to."

He sat on the floor within touching distance of Whizzer and reached out a hand toward the pile. He picked through the top layer and drew out a photograph. "This for instance," he said.

Whizzer looked at the snapshot thoughtfully and then grinned. "That was just an outing, one of the afternoon excursions Bea took Twink on. Pretty tricky business, really. Not for Bea, of course. How hard is riding a bicycle? But see the way Twink is propped in the basket? Wedged in safely with towels and a beach blanket and that paper bag full of sandwiches."

"Where were they going?"

"Just anywhere," Whizzer answered. "It was Bea's idea to show Twink the outside world from the start. It was she who taught Twink about textures of things—sand, grass, leaves, material. Textures and tastes," Whizzer added with a smile. "Like sand in cucumber sandwiches and salt water in a windpipe. And, at the end of an afternoon, sunburn."

She looked thoughtfully at the photograph and turned it over in her hand. "I guess this would be just after they arrived at Parker's. Probably the one trip I didn't take with my folks."

"You mean they took you with them every time?" Harry asked astonished. "Even when there was school?"

Whizzer grinned. "Yep, even then," she said. "I couldn't go on that first visit because just then we couldn't afford it. Parker's and the doctors' bills that had piled up began to take their toll. Mother finally took a deep breath and went to work."

"For cash," said Harry.

"That, and I think to keep her mind off Twink as much as possible. Anyway, I went along on every other trip—from Florida to Arizona to New England and back again."

Whizzer began thumbing through the pieces of paper and photos she'd saved over the years.

"Look at this," she said, handing a color picture to Harry. It was a shot of Bea wrapped in a huge white blanket, sitting in a wagon, carrying some sort of white bottle. Twink, tentatively, stood behind her, wagon handle in hand, balanced. She was dressed all in white and had a nurse's cap perched on her curls.

"One of the super things about Parker's was St. Gordon's Day," said Whizzer. "Dr. Parker, I guess, realized how tiresome a routine life got. Every chance he had he declared holidays, St. Gordon's Days. Gordon was his middle name. There would be fairs, with booths and picnics and contests of all sorts. Or maybe an excursion out onto the water for a day's fishing. Or a movie at night. Something to break the monotony of breakfast-class; lunch-therapy; nap; playtime, dinner-and-bed."

Harry leaned back against a chair and settled in.

"This must have been a costume party," Whizzer continued. "Yes, I'm almost sure it was. Twink went as Bea, and Bea went as Twink. They won first prize, but it was really a tie. The best costume, the funniest one, was worn by five little boys about eight. They came as a giant sort of 'rollapede.' They'd sewn some sheets together and painted them green. There were five head holes cut, and a tail was attached somehow. Lined up in their wheelchairs, their fabulous animal stretched out about twenty feet, I'd say. I can still remember their entrance. It was absolutely super. Five midgets covered by one huge tarpaulin, ice-skating in line."

Whizzer laughed softly to herself and ran her hand through the stack. Harry pictured the mythological rollapede. He agreed with Whizzer that it was more imaginative than Bea and Twink's costume. Of course, those kids were older than Twink was, so it wasn't a fair contest, really.

"Here's a very glum one," Whizzer said, handing Harry another photograph. "That's Twink in class, looking rather puzzled, which was unusual for her. Dr. Brownlee must have said something confusing to her."

"I wonder what," Harry said.

"Who knows," Whizzer shrugged. "Brownlee was the great teacher at Parker's but a real martinet, in his way. He had Twink in class right from the beginning, an early head-start kind of thing. Little kids got used to sitting there, to listening and to trying to follow the work and Brownlee's voice. *That* was important. I listened once to his class and could hardly understand a thing he said. But after a while, the kids themselves got used to it and really did learn a lot."

"How old is Twink there?" Harry asked, pointing to the picture in his hand.

"Maybe three, maybe a little less. She wasn't really old enough to take part in class. But she did try. She would sing along with the others during nursery-rhyme time, making little sing-songy sounds that came as close as she could get them to what she heard. She nodded yes or no when yes-and-no questions were asked. She really listened during story-hour or a lesson. She wasn't going to be cut out of anything just because she was small, not our Twink. A very determined lady she was, even then."

"Here's a picture of you," said Harry, having dug into the pile himself. "When was that?"

"Oh," Whizzer said, taking Harry's hand to steady it as she looked at the photograph. "I was about eight, maybe nine, then. That was our first Christmas with

Twink at Parker's. My first visit there, too, as I recall."

"Was it fun?" Harry asked.

"I don't really remember whether it was or not," Whizzer said, trying to think. "It had good moments and bad ones, I suppose. The good ones were mostly Twinkle's. It was clear she loved that place. She was thriving. She chattered and laughed and even tried to speak, though listening to her was rough going, I do remember. She was standing in her walker and trying to take a few tiny, rather shaky steps. Progress, in other words."

"What were the bad moments, then?" asked Harry. He was conscious of an empty feeling in his stomach. Really, he only wanted to know and believe in Twink's happy ones.

"Well, for one thing," Whizzer recalled, "it was the first time I heard Mother and Daddy talking about money. In a worried way, I mean. This was long before Daddy left his job and started on his own, and ages before he finally got to be really successful. None of this was cheap, and dragging me along—though the reasoning was O.K.—wasn't making things any easier. But that wasn't really a 'bad' moment. There was only one of those, and that one just kept recurring. There were more than one hundred kids in the school. But no more than six families arrived to spend Christmas with them. Ninety-four kids, Harry, had purposely been hidden away, forgotten. They were embarrassments, I guess. It was then that Mother and Daddy decided never to let Twink spend Christmas alone. No matter what."

Harry was silent, thinking.

"And you know what?" Whizzer said. "She never had to."

# Chapter Three

"Listen, Harry," Whizzer said after a quiet moment. "We can talk about this tomorrow. Or some other time. Maybe you're tired. It must have been a pretty long day for you."

Harry sat up straight and smiled, with just a little effort. "I'm fine," he said hurriedly. "Really. I do want to hear about

Twink. About her and you and everything."

"Well," Whizzer said slowly, "if you do get fed up or exhausted or anything, just say so."

"I'll be fine. It's only just twelve," Harry noted, looking at his watch.

"Well, I'll go on as long as you can stand it," Whizzer announced. "I'll just flip through all this stuff and mention what seems important. Most of it is in order, but I imagine you can put it all together later if something sticks out."

"I'll probably be up all night putting it in order," Harry admitted.

Whizzer took a big breath and smiled. She closed her eyes, put out her right hand, and let her fingers scavenge in the papers before her. She drew out another snapshot.

Lucia. Lucia Rodriguez y Cruz. One of Twink's best friends at Parker's. A cute little thing from Caracas, maybe a year older than Twink and not so severely handicapped.

Between Twink and Lucia an extrasensory kind of understanding had grown. In class, when Twink knew the answer to one of Dr. Brownlee's questions, she often got so excited that she couldn't, in her own way, announce she knew what she did. Lucia somehow sensed these moments. It was she who sat nearby and who raised Twink's hand for her.

Dr. Parker's train. Three special cars in which the entire school traveled from north to south and back again.

Dr. Parker had leased on a long-term basis two large homes in East Hampton, New York. During the summer, when Florida became unbearably humid, life on Long Island was cool, fun, and a little more frantic.

Making these moves wasn't easy. It meant more than just moving children, staff, and clothing. It meant moving physical therapy equipment, toys, games, food— and animals.

For Parker's was more than a home for handicapped kids. Over the years it had grown into an unofficial Animal Rescue League. There were five cocker spaniels, named after five of Mr. Disney's dwarfs, Grumpy and Sneezy excepted. There was a trained rabbit named Nosey, donated by a passing magician who had come to entertain one St. Gordon's Day long ago. There was one deodorized skunk. Four tanks of tropical fish. A plastic flamingo to put on the lawn. Two alley cats named Hermione and Herman that had wandered across the school's property and stayed. And there was one pony named Lindy.

Loading for each trip took several days. Cooks prepared whole turkeys and roast beefs. They baked bread, put up preserves, sliced tons of cabbages for coleslaw, made whole gallons of Kool-Aid. All this was carefully prepared, wrapped, and loaded into three cars that sat on a railroad spur not far from either house. A buffet was arranged in the men's room of one car. A kitchen was organized in the ladies' room of the next.

When everything was ready and the kids had been helped onto the train and settled, the locomotive that would take them north or south detached itself from a passenger train standing in a nearby station. The shock of cars hitting one another delighted everyone. Summer, or winter, had arrived.

Jesus. Jesus something. From Buenos Aires. Looked like an elf and had a marvelous, tricky sense of humor. Each time the school moved from Florida to Long Island, or the other way around, as soon as he arrived Jesus would send a telegram to his family. It always said the same thing. "Jesus has arrived safe and sound."

Jack Watson, eleven, and Lindy.
The pony was Jack's life. He brushed her daily, made certain she had food and water in her troughs. He polished her bridle and saddle. He liked to tie colorful ribbons in her mane.

Twink, aged four, on her special tricycle. There were straps attached to the pedals so that her feet would fit in and stay in. She wasn't expert at pedaling, but she did love it.

Twink, aged seven, standing in her walker. By this time she had progressed so well she was able to walk without aid some twenty or thirty steps at a time. Also, by this time, she had discovered reading.

Chas Chase, another of Twink's friends, at eight. A real mischief-maker. His therapy sessions were water fights and kicking matches. He loved to throw speech therapy classes into an uproar by salting his practice sentences with marvelous new words he'd learned. The words were gen-

erally made up of from four to seven letters.

Jack Watson again, looking very determined and in charge of Lindy who was
attached to the school's pony cart.

One year, on the night before the school
was to leave for Florida and a warm winter, Jack crept out of bed at about nine
o'clock. He had decided to take Lindy to
the station on his own, all by himself. She
was "his" pony. She should be handled by
no one else. Everyone was to know he
could take care of her under any circum-
stances.

It wasn't an easy trip. Jack walked without the aid of a walker, his legs operating
in scissor fashion, one leg nearly revolving
around the other as he laboriously made
his way from place to place. His arms were
under better control: he needed only to
concentrate on the desired movement to
get the desired response. He was fine as
long as he had time to think and to plan.

Jack slipped out of the dormitory and
made his way as quietly as he could to the
little stable. He took Lindy's bridle and a
handful of oats which he stuck into his
pocket. He left her night blanket on,
slipped the bridle over her head and the

bit into her mouth with some difficulty, and led her out. He tip-toed, in his own fashion, down the long drive and out into the road, leading his pony toward East Hampton, five miles away.

Traffic on the road to the railroad station that night was light. No one seemed to think it strange to see a pony led by a cripple alone on the road. Jack didn't think it was strange, either. He carefully stayed on the left side of the road, swinging one leg round the other, moving forward slowly. Lindy lazed behind, nibbling roadside greenery when Jack stopped to rest.

By midnight he had reached the halfway point in his journey. He pulled Lindy off the road and into some trees, feeding her the oats he had thoughtfully brought with him. The train would leave at seven. He had an easy six hours before he felt he had to arrive for the loading.

One o'clock found him struggling past the outlying houses of the town, Lindy's hooves making sleepy clip-clops on the pavement as he crossed a five-way intersection. Jack stopped under a street-light. The heat from the lamp above was warm and comforting.

Half a mile from the railroad station, an

all-night trucker pulled out from a driveway, startling both Jack and Lindy. Jack nearly fell over as Lindy pulled at the bridle he held, but he hung on and calmed her, pushing determinedly on.

But Lindy was fully awake then, and nervous. She pulled up from time to time, starting to back and balk, turning her head toward the Parker houses longingly.

A hundred yards from the station, Lindy pulled up short. She pulled up fast and short and strong. Jack tilted backward, losing his balance, letting go the reins he had held so tightly for five hours. As he fell, Lindy wheeled around and headed home, cantering happily in the cool autumn night air, leaving Jack alone on the pavement, a little dazed and definitely bewildered to see all his work and effort so easily ruined.

He picked himself up slowly, and even more slowly swung his left foot around his right, heading home, trailing the pony who soon was miles ahead of him. His speed homeward was a little slower than it had been coming into town, but he walked with a quiet little smile on his face.

He had almost done it. It was his first independent journey. He had nearly been successful. After all, Lindy weighed a great deal more than he did.

Jack had had a real experience.


Here's another picture, one that really wrecks me. Sally Losey, eleven or perhaps twelve, depressed and unhappy in her wheelchair. She had just found out about sex. And marriage and love.

Charles Neill, nearly eighteen, graduating. He was one of the lucky few who had grown strong enough, and secure enough, to face the outside world. Most kids had to go on to other institutions. A few went home. The smile on Charles' face shows he knows how lucky he was; the way he clutches his hands together how terrified of his first steps outside.


Dr. and Mrs. Parker, in Florida, when he came back from the hospital. He had nearly died from pneumonia. Just before the school had to close.


Twink, about eight, at the airport in Chicago, arriving home for her first real visit.

# Chapter Four

"Her first visit, in all that time?" Harry asked. "In six years?"

Whizzer nodded. "Mother and Daddy had wanted her home before then, but Dr. Parker never gave his O.K. And he was probably right. He felt his kids needed all the practice and training they could get— and as little spoiling as possible."

"How could Twink ever have been spoiled?"

"You'd be surprised," Whizzer smiled. "Just by listening to other people sometimes can do it."

The visit started out well enough. Twink wasn't a baby any more. We could talk to her and reason, play with her and not worry quite so much. Bea got her unpacked and organized, and then left for a holiday.

When we were all at home, things were fine. Mother had bought a secondhand piano for Twink to pound on. She'd developed a definite rhythm and a terrific love for music of all kinds: jazz, classical, the beginnings of rock. Twink had a closetful of new clothes. And we had all the books I had loved at her age. Our first full day together was quite a success.

But Twink already had a reputation to uphold. Mother and Daddy had talked about her for such a long time, about how fast she was growing and learning and just generally coming along that all their friends, and of course the family, had to visit. And no matter how well *we* thought she was doing, in the eyes of everyone else she was still a shock. A tiny, undernourished-looking kid huddled in steel and leather, or standing surrounded by shiny metal that was cruel to the eye.

Twink, of course, knew how people felt. She heard it in their voices, those raised tones people use when they're certain someone is deaf, blind, or foreign. And some people tried too hard, made too much of Twink. She wasn't used to being praised for every little thing. Or told how nice she looked, or how well she managed her walker.

One evening we all went downtown to Daddy's club for dinner. Mother had telephoned ahead and told the manager what we were doing, asking that an elevator and a wheelchair be ready.

Twink was dressed beautifully that night. And she *was* a pretty little girl. We looked a little alike, then. Daddy carried her into the club's lobby. The chair was ready and the elevator was waiting. We all rode up confidently, terribly proud of ourselves, a family at last.

We wheeled Twink into a dining room on the fourth floor. We deliberately took a corner table. Mother and Daddy had thought ahead and realized a few people might be upset by seeing us feed Twink. We had taken every precaution we could think of to make certain she had a lovely evening out.

And we did have a good time. The food was wonderful. Twink was enjoying herself. Daddy fed her very carefully, with small bites to minimize the chances of any kind of accident. He would look across the table at me or at Mother every so often, and wink. We winked back.

The maitre d' appeared from nowhere. Had we finished? Would we mind hurrying a little? We were making it difficult for other members and guests to dine comfortably.

We had been so intense in our corner we hadn't noticed how many people there were around us, sitting in silence, staring. I looked around and nearly died from embarrassment. Then I got mad.

Mother got mad, too, but faster and with more power. Daddy could see she was about to let the whole room have it at the top of her lungs. He touched her arm as he told the maitre d' we had nearly finished and would leave in a few more minutes.

But then, of course, we couldn't just slip out. We had to weave through all the tables, pushing Twink's chair. I'll never forget the look on Mother's face as she threaded her way through members and guests, memorizing every face in the room, drawing up lists of whole families never to see or speak with again.

On the way home, as we drove up Michigan Avenue, Twink spelled out a thank you. She had a wonderful time, she said. The club was so beautiful.

# Chapter Five

This is the first picture I ever took of a sunset in Arizona. I've only taken maybe two thousand others since then.

This was near the school the McGraws ran for C.P.'s, where Twink went when she was eight. It looked perfect: sunshine and no humidity, desert flowers and an attractive building to live in. Just before Bea was married, she took Twink down there.

The three of us landing at the Phoenix Airport, seven months after Dr. Parker had had to retire. It was our first weekend visit with Twink.

The McGraws, Dr. and wife, Mary. He wasn't around much. She was scared to death of the twenty kids they had. She spent her whole life in her own house about four hundred yards up the road from school.

The first picture I took of Twink there. She was in a wheelchair because her walker had been lost. A new one was supposed to be on its way.

Juliet Bell, aged five. The daughter of one of the two attendants at McGraw's. A sort of mascot. She made everyone feel good. She was terribly cute, always in motion, and fantastically intense about helping her mother at the center. She bustled from chair to bed, fluffing pillows and getting books, feeding ice cream, chattering all the time like a miniature mother. The McGraws could have learned from her.

Mother in her new office. When Twink went to Phoenix, the bills went up and Mother had to get a better-paying job. I used to visit her there once in a while, after school.

A picture of Twink amid the books in her library. She was never any good at arithmetic, but she was terrific at spelling.

In the background, there, you can see the center's color television set, relied on pretty heavily. Educational television during the day; commercial shows at night. To keep the kids occupied, because the McGraws seemed to be having a lot of trouble hiring proper help. There were no real classes during the day.

Given and Kevin Wood, who shared Twink's room. Twins from Minneapolis.

Dr. McGraw again, on another of our visits. He seemed like a kind man, a little vague at times. He was always off somewhere making speeches. Sometimes he would be gone for four or five days in a row, come back for a weekend, go off again.

Twink at nine. Much thinner now, and very pale despite the Arizona sun. Her walker had never been replaced. Also, for some reason, all the clothes Mother sent her were never to be found on visits. Twink began to have cavities about this time. Mother began to have nervous, sleepless nights. Daddy began writing to other schools.

Twink's tenth birthday weekend. New cardigans, skirts, books and jewelry, an electric page-turner so she could read more quickly and with less effort. A portable phonograph with records by Errol Garner, Brubeck, Duke Ellington, Peter Nero.

Twink having dinner at McGraw's. That's Juliet's mother sitting in the circle, rotating as quickly and efficiently as she could. She fed one child after another, shoveling down each throat a sort of corn mash and chopped bacon. Twink is there, the fourth on the left. Mostly, Twink had been feeding herself for almost four years before this.

Dr. and Mrs. McGraw, Daddy and Mother playing bridge, which they did a lot. It was Twink's eleventh birthday weekend. Mother finally came away from the bridge table convinced she knew what Dr. McGraw really did all the time he was supposed to be away lecturing. Bridge tournaments.

Me, the last time I visited Twink in Arizona. Dr. McGraw had returned late that Saturday night, all smiles. He was delighted to see us.

Mother jumped right in. "How close

are you," she said, "in master points? If you play half as well at the tournaments as you do here . . ."

"Well," Dr. McGraw thought, looking a little proud, "this last trip brings me within about——" He stopped abruptly, caught.

"Doubtless," Daddy said very slowly, "you also learned a little something to benefit the children here. A new technique or exercise? Perhaps you even found some qualified people to work here, at last."

The doctor was nervous. "Surely," he said, "you don't begrudge a man his hobby? It really hurts no one, now, does it?"

"Does it help anyone?" Mother asked quickly.

Dr. McGraw looked at us for a moment, recovering. "It doesn't, you're right," he said. "But when you have so many difficult responsibilities . . . now, Twink, for instance, isn't the easiest child we have here."

Mother's mouth opened in astonishment. Daddy just waited.

"Frequently we have to let children go. Sometimes they damage the progress of others. Of course, it's difficult to say that Twink would become unmanageable. But in some cases, we have no choice." He paused for a moment. "Either we raise tuition for all the children to cover additional staff and supply expense, or we have to send a child somewhere else."

We all stared at McGraw. Then Daddy said something about the weather or about the desert spring, and we got out of there.

Mother said she felt like Bonnie Parker without her shotgun.


"But what happened?" Harry asked. "I mean, after that."

"Nothing," Whizzer answered. "That's one of life's little jokes. There are only about four decent places in the whole country for people like Twink. We couldn't afford to get mad."

"But that's just plain blackma——," Harry said.

Whizzer nodded and cut him off. "True," she said. "You always have to think what is most important—Twink, or seeing someone get what he deserves."


Here's me and Daddy, two long tall drinks of water at O'Hare Field. Mother took the picture as Daddy was flying off to California to look at another place for Twink. Two weeks later the place folded.

Twink, at the airport, home for a few days on her way to New England. A couple of things here. One, she's clutching a copy of *Life*. That's how she found out about Oxford Mountain. That's how *we* found out about it.

Two, she's in pretty bad shape. Her leg muscles had sort of died, from lack of exercise and treatment. She was wearing full braces then, on her legs and on her back. They fit badly, and they should have aggravated her to tears. They didn't.

There was nothing to be done. The McGraws weren't stupid. They had food bills and receipts for equipment, and tax statements for the few employees they had. They *had* provided care. Of a sort.

Twink, at home, laughing. Daddy is laughing, too. Twink had a favorite joke, even though it took hours to spell out. "What does a firefly say when he backs into an electric fan?" "I'm de-lighted!"

At her feet are a few of her books and magazines: *Life, Time, The New Yorker;* Hemingway, Fitzgerald, Rosemary Sutcliffe, Dickens, the Bible. Also a lot of movie magazines. She was Hollywood's Number One Fan.

Twink, all dressed up to go to the airport again, on her way to Oxford Mountain. That was the day she told me about her ambition. She had decided to be a writer. She had been reading the lives of famous women, women who had struggled to overcome prejudice, hardship, and handicaps. Women who grew into responsible, exciting personalities with something to give to mankind. Twink had already decided what story she would tell, and what she would give to the world. We agreed her story would take a long time to tell. But Twink thought that was probably all to the good. There would be few mistakes then.

# Chapter Six

"Night, kids," Kenneth said, standing in the doorway. "See you in the morning."

Harry looked up and waved his goodnight. Whizzer turned around and blew

Kenneth a kiss. Harry waited until she had turned around again to face him.

"For someone who's mostly stationary," he said, "Twink sure got around."

"Not always because she wanted to," Whizzer admitted. "If there were more schools, more well-trained people, Twink could have skipped the McGraw bit altogether. And there are a few things," she continued, "Twink could well have afforded to miss."

Harry, catching Whizzer's tone and thinking about the accident, shut up.

Whizzer sighed and sat up straight. She tried out a small smile, and reached down once again into the pile of things before her.

Tommy Stoddard, at Oxford Mountain. His father was a famous eye doctor in Boston. Tommy was an intern at Mass General Hosptial, on leave to work for six months at Oxford. I had a crush on him for two and a half years.

Oxford, a distance shot in late afternoon, Thanksgiving of Twink's first year there. It was better equipped, better run, and more fun that McGraw's desert hideaway. Situated in the mountains of western Massachusetts, Oxford was not just for

people like Twink. There was a program
for the deaf, and one for the blind. And
there was a day school for handicapped
kids who lived in neighboring towns. A
place where the emphasis was on de-
veloping that part of the child not damaged: his brain.

Dr. William Wallace, the retired sur-
geon who directed the programs at Oxford.
He was an old, bright, enthusiastic man
who cared. He recruited his staff from Boston hospitals. *It* was young, bright, and
enthusiastic. He had a favorite picture in
his office: a girl, not much older than
Twink was then, skiing down a slight,
snow-covered slope—in her wheelchair.
One of the staff had built a sled for her
that could be controlled electrically.

Oxford Mountain was a happy place.
Then.

Tommy Stoddard again, with the
typewriter he made for Twink. It was a
portable electric that he had rented. For
more than a week he worked on it, arrang-
ing with wire and wood to make each key
on the keyboard bigger. Each key had a
larger wooden key of the same character
fitted over it. Twink was able to begin
typing then, in her swooping fashion. Her

arm swung across and above the keyboard; then her hand would dive downward toward the general area of the key she wanted to use. Her control was pretty good. Words might be misspelled, but not by much.

The first paragraphs of Twink's first story. It was supposed to be about a girl who was handicapped. The girl had been ill all her life but still found every day full of fun. Twink said that the girl's story wasn't anything like her own, only some things would seem similar.

"Caroline opened her eyes and smiled at the sunshine. She could see and hear the birds outside her window.

" 'Thank you, God,' she said aloud, 'for another day.' "

Twink's first birthday at Oxford Mountain, her twelfth. The one weekend when everyone was happy. Twink seemed more alive than she had in years. She was comfortable, she was having fun again. Dr. Wallace said he was impressed with her mind and her concentration. Tommy Stoddard told us he was extending his internship there. He had begun to wonder if perhaps he ought to specialize in cerebral palsy and its treatment rather than in brain surgery.

A letter, about one month later, from Dr. Wallace.

Dear Mr. and Mrs. Munson:

I do not mean to alarm you unduly, but within the past weeks a change has occurred in Twink's condition.

Spasms that she has thus far controlled are becoming stronger. Eating is more difficult. Dressing has become a daily "battle." Her studies have begun being interrupted by sudden movements new and strange to us.

Frankly, all of us here are a bit puzzled. True, we know cerebral palsy is a generally debilitating disease. That those who suffer from it do not expect as long or as happy a life as others. And that changes do, from time to time, occur.

It begins to seem to us here that unless these changes cease in a very short time, we will have to recommend a series of operations that are designed to minimize these sudden, new movements. Simple enough, the operations entail severing some tendons that are now beginning to pull in unexpected ways. Although it might mean Twink would be less able to do things for herself, it would also mean she would have people around who could do these same things for her more efficiently.

It is, of course, too early to recommend with confidence. I simply wanted you to know, so that in future, whatever action we all take together comes as no surprise or shock.

I look forward to your next visit.

Sincerely,

(signed) Dr. William Wallace.

These are pages of an article from a medical journal that Tommy and Twink discovered at about the same time. One of a series about an operation called "chemo-paledectomy."

While only experimental, the operation seemed at that time to hold hope for people with palsy. Doctors would drill a small hole in a patient's skull. Then one drop of alcohol was allowed to fall through the opening. The portion of the brain the alcohol hit would then be frozen in a way that lessened shaking and involuntary actions.

The side effects and the permanence of the operation were still in doubt. Twink and Tommy waited eagerly for each new issue of the magazine.

All of us at Easter that year. We are all smiling. I can't remember why.

That was the weekend that Mother and Daddy told Dr. Wallace they would never allow any operation that would make Twink less than she was. It was also the weekend that Twink and Tommy sprung their medical research on us all.

Twink implored Daddy to investigate the operation. To see the doctor about whom she had been reading. She persisted even though we all pointed out that the operation was only experimental. She stood her ground. Tommy stood with her. Twink spelled it out for us. "It's even more important," she said, "because it is experimental. This might be a way of helping others."

Twink told me, when we were alone, that she desperately wanted Caroline's story to have a happy ending.

A page from my own diary, not very long after that. Mother and Daddy were in New York, tracking down the man who was experimenting with his drops of alcohol.

even if Tommy does walk like a duck and his skin is much too white, he's still the most beautiful, sexy man I've ever seen. I wonder what he thinks of me. Does he at all?

Had a long, difficult session with Twink. About God. I can understand why she says what she does, and how she absolutely has to believe in Him. But it burns me just the same.

For myself, looking at Twink, it's impossible to believe in Him at all. He must be so cruel, if He exists, to do this to her. What possible sense can there be in it? None! But of course I couldn't say that to her. She *has* to believe there's a pattern of some kind, a divine plan into which she fits somewhere. Reincarnation would be super, but she doesn't go that far. That way, at least, she would possibly have been someone whole and happy before and still might be in another life. Twink *insists* that because she can at any rate *see*, He must want her to see clearly, to observe, and to write about what she sees honestly. Without pretending anything, without making anything too pretty.

Damn it, there's absolutely, totally nothing pretty in her life! If there is a God, I say He's a rotten one, and doesn't deserve her kind of devotion! Damn it, damn it, damn *Him!* How I admire her! God, how I do!

# Chapter Seven

A letter from Twink to Mother and Daddy. I don't know whether I kept it because it's from Twink, or because Tommy Stoddard wrote it for her.

Dear Mummy and Daddy:

I am not upset about the doctor in New York. He's probably right about my not being old enough for what he does. Thank you, anyway, for trying.

The wonderful thing is he at least told you about Dr. Fry. Even though what he does is different, maybe he's our man. I do hope so. Could you telephone me after you've talked to him?

Today I finished reading "Gone with the Wind." There must be things I

don't quite understand, but I liked it anyway. I hope they bring the movie back now. Isn't Melanie wonderful?
Love from Twink (and Tommy)

From my diary, a few weeks later.

something that makes me uneasy. Maybe Dr. Fry sounds too glib. It's probably that he's too busy to seem human. But I'm glad Daddy asked the questions he did. What a terrible thing it would be if Twink's hearing or vision or the small control she has left should suddenly desert her. One thing anyway is nice: at least she'll be close to home all that time.

The report from the Illinois Medical Society on the qualifications of Dr. Joseph Fry. All in order. All perfectly O.K.

The ticket stubs from Twink's flight from Boston to Chicago before the operation. Also those of Tommy Stoddard, who volunteered to come with her, to keep her company. Tommy stayed for a few days, but had to leave the night before the operation began.

My diary again, although I can't think why I kept this page. I guess it had to do with Twink's brief stay at home before going into the hospital.

anyway, in the elevator, Mother had finally had enough. She suggested quietly to the woman how grateful we all must be that her husband was obviously the better part of *that* marriage, since *he* hadn't hesitated to help Twink. Mother even went so far as to ask the woman whether the four children she mentioned were her husband's from a previous marriage!

Mother gets mean when she's defensive.

A short note from Tommy, left on the front door of our apartment.

Whizzer—have gone to hospital with family to help Twink settle in for the tests. Come when you can. T.

During the few days Tommy was around, Twink had to go through a series of tests to determine her strength, her reflexes, her blood type, her ability to withstand surgery without anesthesia since she was only just thirteen.

It was then we were told exactly what the operation meant. Twink, I think, wanted the thing so badly she never really heard what the doctor said.

On the day before the operation itself, Twink was to spend several hours in the operating theater. Her head was to be entirely shaved. After she had been securely attached to the operating table, two holes would be bored in her head—one in the front of her skull, the other at its base. These were to allow a brace to be screwed into her head, making her absolutely still so she couldn't suddenly move or pull away from what followed.

Immobile, Twink would be fed a particular kind of blue dye which would enable the technicians to X-ray her skull, locating as precisely as possible the area of the brain that would later receive sonic waves.

During the operation on the second day, and after the doctors had exposed Twink's brain, she would be asked to follow certain commands. Moving a hand, for example, or holding up a certain number of fingers, or pointing. These commands and Twink's ability to respond were the reasons the surgery would be performed without pain-killing drugs or any kind of anesthesia.

Tommy sat quietly between Twink and myself, listening and nodding. Even when Mother and Daddy begged Twink not to go ahead, she could not be dissuaded. Daddy mentioned everything he could think of—except the actual physical pain—to convince Twink not to go along as planned. He told her what the doctor had forgotten: there would have to be two identical operations, one for each side of the brain.

Twink wouldn't give in. Her reasoning was simple. Having gone through the first operation, the second would be that much easier since she would know exactly what to expect. The operations couldn't leave her worse off than before, and there *was* a chance she would be improved. How could science progress unless people were willing to take chances?

We all left the hospital that night with fear and pride. Fear of the unknown for Twink's sake. Pride in Twink for knowing what she wanted and sticking to it.

An old page from my desk calendar, the one for the day of the first operation. I didn't know what to write on it, so I left it absolutely blank.

We arrived at the hospital at dawn and sat waiting with Twink, reading the morning newspapers and killing time. At seven a nurse came in with clippers, comb, and an electric razor. Twink was dying to see what she looked like without hair. She spelled that it was like being born again, only this time she'd know what she looked like from the very beginning.

After her head was wrapped in sterile gauze, a wheelchair was brought to her bedside. Daddy helped her into it. We all walked down the hall with her. We stopped near the doors of the operating room. We kissed her good luck.

The doctor, before he went into the operating theater, told us again what was to happen that first day. He explained that the skull itself was only bone and largely without nerves. The only blood would come from breaking the skin before the doctors reached the skull itself.

We waited outside, pacing around the hallways, leaving once in a while for coffee in a cafeteria on another floor. Mother tried to read. Daddy balanced two checking accounts. I looked out a window and got a headache from staring at the sun.

A few hours later a nurse came to ask us to return to Twink's room. She thought we might prefer to see her in privacy, which was only customary. I had an instant sensation: they were terrified we would get hysterical when we first saw her, that we might frighten other families and friends in the area waiting for other patients to return.

I was right. When Twink was wheeled in, we all gasped in spite of ourselves. Though her head was neatly bandaged, the bandage was turning color before our eyes. The red was very red against the white gauze. Starker still against the terrible pallor of Twink's face.

Daddy helped an orderly prop Twink up in bed. She tried to smile at us all, but it hurt too much. The orderly strapped her in an upright position, tying a canvas belt across her chest. He adjusted a dozen pillows around her neck and at the back of her head, and cautioned us about letting Twink move her head in any direction too suddenly.

Twink sat motionless for a moment. Then her hands moved, agitatedly. She wanted to spell something. Mother and Daddy stood on either side of her bed, each holding one of her hands. It took us nearly twenty minutes to piece Twink's thought together.

"I will only say this once," she said. "It hurts, terribly." Tears began to streak down her face then, but she wouldn't allow herself to really cry, to sob and perhaps move her head. Mother grit her own teeth. I had to turn away.

"Do you want to continue, darling?" Daddy asked her. "You don't have to, you know. It's not too late to stop."

I turned. Twink nodded her head a fraction of an inch. She wanted to continue. I turned away again, bleary-eyed.

Everything was silent then. Daddy held Twink's hand. Mother came over to me and put her arm around my shoulders.

"Ellie!" Daddy said under his breath. Mother turned around an instant before I did.

"Oh God!" she choked, and ran from the room.

Twink was straining against her bonds. She was vomiting blue dye.

# Chapter Eight

I went home for the night. Mother and Daddy stayed at the hospital, without sleep. Twink retched regularly. She was allowed neither food nor a sedative to help her sleep. The hospital worried that with sedation, she might choke if she became ill again.

I arrived at dawn. Twink had been cleaned up. She felt a little stronger. We went together, the four of us, down that hall again, toward the operating room. She tried to wave back at us encouragingly. The doors swung closed behind her wheelchair.

And we had another three hours to ourselves. Mother and Daddy went back to Twink's room to shower and change. I just mooned around. Then we had breakfast in the cafeteria, and finished again with too much time to waste.

We decided to wait in Twink's room. But once we got there, there was nothing to do. Finally, we tried to picture the operation taking place. It seemed so simple. A large flap of skin was cut away from Twink's skull, over her right ear. The skull was cleansed, then a section sawed away and pulled out. The brain would be sitting quietly, waiting.

The doctor would bring up whatever machine it was that sent out ultrasonic waves, and direct it at the part of the brain that controlled Twink's responses on her left side. Certain that everything was ready and everything in place, he would push a button or pull a lever, somehow sending sound waves into Twink's brain a little at a time. He would ask her to move something . . . perhaps her left hand. Hold up two fingers, he might say. Or wave your hand from right to left. Make a fist. Can you wiggle your toes on your left foot?

When Twink could respond to everything as directed, she would be bandaged again and wheeled out. The time between this operation and the one on the left side of her brain depended on how fast Twink's strength returned.

A nurse came to tell us Twink was on her way. "Remember," said Daddy to us.

"We all promised to be cheerful and talkative and hopeful. No matter how she looks."

This is the first "after" picture, just when Twink came home from the hospital.

You can see she's not smiling. All she really wanted was to be left alone, to rest. The pain, she said, was gradually easing. But she didn't feel like doing anything much, at least not for a while.

Mother and Daddy talked to Fry about Twink's depression. He said it was rather normal and not to bug her. So we didn't. Daddy went back to work. Mother took a leave of absence from her job to spend as much time as she could with Twink, and started buying things for her: new records, new clothes, a new series of books about famous British women.

Twink's copy of *Winnie-the-Pooh*. About two months after the operation, Twink snapped back to life. Mother read this to her, every afternoon, and Twink just loved it.

She also loved watching television but only for a short time. Her eyes, she said, tired a little too easily. She answered get-well cards by spelling her messages out to Mother or me. She sat at her window and watched the city below. She napped.

Twink and Tommy Stoddard, on one of his two weekend visits. This was at least three months after she'd come home and she really was more like her old self. But better. The operation had already begun to have a good effect. Twink's sudden movements on her left side were few and far between. She seemed more composed, more comfortable. And she was somehow prettier, too.

She laughed a lot and began to outline her book. Tommy took her for mad spins around the neighborhood, pretending Twink was a slalom racer on wheels.

A postcard I bought in the hospital's tobacco shop the day Twink went in for a routine examination.

That was the day, according to my diary, that Dr. Fry seemed to me a true cold fish. Daddy had asked him about Twink's vision which, she said, was blurry from time to time.

"That's to be expected," Fry said. "An after-effect, I suppose. It should wear off in time."

118

"I hope so," said Daddy. "Otherwise, we can't allow Twink to have the second operation."

"Well," said Fry, pulling himself up, "I understand your worry. But insofar as the first operation seems so much more successful than anyone had hoped, I assume you want to do whatever else you can to improve her health."

Before Daddy could even answer, Fry was moving efficiently down the hall, white coat flapping about his knees.

My dairy, the day of the second operation. Very brief.

Daddy promised Twink this morning an evening at the Drake ballroom as soon as she felt like it. Wouldn't that be wonderful!

A picture of Oxford Mountain under a huge gray quilt of snow. Tommy sent it to Twink and asked how she was doing.

But there wasn't much to report. For months after the second operation, Twink was listless. She didn't seem to care about anything. There was a new line on her forehead that I used to tease her about. A worry line, I called it, and accused her of plotting to take her first steps some dark, stormy night when everyone was asleep.

And I imagine she *was* worried. She'd had both operations by then. She couldn't help but wonder about their effects.

Here's a rather blurry shot of a Sunday outing, with Mother, Daddy, and Twink. We used to take Twink out every week for a drive along Lake Shore Drive.

It was on one of these outings, about a week or two later, that Twink, in the front seat and well-propped up, began slipping down, falling on her right side. Daddy pulled the car over, got out, and rearranged Twink, propping her up more securely. Twink smiled thank you and off we drove.

Within minutes, Twink had fallen toward the car door again.

"What's the matter?" I said.

Twink didn't answer. She shook her head. She didn't know what was happening, either.

"Is it the way you're loaded?" Daddy asked.

"Is it your back?" Mother said.

Twink said she didn't know.

Within minutes Daddy had driven to the emergency entrance of the hospital. For something had gone wrong. The second operation had either been too little or too much. Twink's muscles, in her back and on her right side, weren't as strong as they had been. Her spasms on the right hadn't decreased as they had on the left after the first operation. Instead of being mobile, Twink's arm and leg on the right were rigid.

All this we discovered as Twink went through four days of new tests. Fry wanted her hospitalized to rest after the rush of an emergency entrance and the exhausting examinations. Daddy wasn't inclined to be too patient, but there was nothing he could do.

So we visited Twink every day in the afternoon. We told her the news and read to her. We brought her foolish little things, like candy and ice cream and a very glamorous pair of shades. We joked and tried to make her smile and laugh. We played word games. In the middle of one of these, Twink interrupted. She spelled very slowly.

"I'm having trouble seeing, Mummy," she spelled.

"How do you mean?" Mother paled. "Cloudy, like before?"

"Yes," Twink spelled. "I can see when it's light, and I can see when it's dark. But I'm afraid I can't see anything else."

We all sat still, absolutely, in shock.

"Mmm . . . ?" Twink said.

"I'm right here, dear," Mother answered.

"Dr. Fry," spelled Twink.

"Of course," Mother said, standing up quickly and looking rather wild as she threw her coat over her shoulders. She was half out of the room before Twink called her. She stopped and went calmly back to the bedside. Twink spelled; Mother waited.

"It's probably only temporary," said Twink. "Don't worry. I just thought you ought to know."

"All right, dear, I won't worry," Mother said. "I'll be back in a minute."

She walked very carefully and very slowly toward the door. Once outside, in the hall, you could hear her footsteps hit full stride in seconds.

Of course Twink was blind.

Twink's old Bible, the one she used to be able to read herself.

122

A page from my dairy.

that difference, at least. Helen Keller
had control of her hands. She could
be taught Braille. Twink doesn't even
have that, now. I don't think I can
read another chapter of that lady's
book to Twink without crying. I can
*see* her grasping at details, grabbing
for hope.

A page from a letter Daddy wrote me,
when he first went up to the Annandale
Clinic.

a diagnosis within a few more days. I
don't imagine there's anything really
serious wrong with me, so don't you
start imagining things.

Your mother and I talked with Dr.
Stoddard last night. He said that
there's nothing organically wrong
with Twink's eyes. They focus and
move as they should. But somehow,
during the operations, the optic nerves
which thread back into the brain were
either damaged by the sonic waves or
severed, so that Twink's brain no
longer receives the right signals from
up front.

Although I *know* it doesn't help Twink any, or undo the accident, all I hope for now is that the Medical Society acts.

A newspaper clipping about Fry's dismissal from University Hospital. His medical license was revoked unconditionally.

I'll never forget what he said the last time we saw him. "Well, how do you expect us to learn if we don't experiment? I warned you, you know."

# Chapter Nine

Harry stood up and went to the bar for another drink. "There are some rotten people around, aren't there?"

Whizzer smiled. "I'll have one of those, too, whatever it is."

Harry brought both drinks back to the floor in front of the fireplace and placed them gently on the carpet. "How long," he said tentatively, "was that before your father died?"

"I guess about six months. Maybe it's terrible to say, but Daddy's death brought Twink back to life, in a way."

"I would have thought it would have wiped her out once and for all."

Whizzer laughed softly. "Harry, after all this time, you still don't understand. *Nothing* can wipe Twink out. Absolutely nothing."

"Well, what about your father?"

"Twink was crushed. She *had* to be. But she soared afterward. She began to worry about Mother. She insisted that she be moved from Oxford to where she is now, Christmastree Hill. To be closer. To help Mother, if she could. It was the same sort of reaction she had later when Mother married your father. Twink was so excited Mother would be taken care of again she could hardly stand it. She thought it was wonderful."

"Crap!" Harry said sharply. "Didn't she ever get mad at anybody?"

Whizzer laughed. "Once," she said, "but you really couldn't say she was mean or anything. Just a little sensitive."

"I can't stand it," Harry said eagerly. "Tell me, tell me!"

"Well," Whizzer began, "Virginia and Ed hired a business manager for Christmastree Hill a few months ago. She was a nice young woman, who I'd guess was great with figures and rotten with kids. She was terrified of them."

"But how could Twink tell?" Harry asked.

"She just could. She sensed it. She knew she was right in her own special way."

"Yes?"

"Yes. Mother and Kenneth went down one weekend for a visit. Twink said she had something to spell. What it was, was that she could tell the business manager was scared, and she thought it was having an effect on some of the littler kids. Twink said she knew the woman was frightened because she could never bring herself to touch any of the children there."

"But that hasn't anything to do with her job," Harry said.

"True enough," Whizzer agreed. "But for the kids who could see, she made life uneasy. She made them feel ugly and dirty. Twink was very, very angry. I guess liking people has less to do with seeing or hearing or speaking than with guts. This lady just didn't have them."

"Did she leave?"

"Within two weeks."

Whizzer stood up and lifted first one pile of papers and photos into her arms, and then the other. "Wait a minute," she said, finding a piece of paper folded carefully at the bottom of the second batch. "Here's something that might interest you."

"What?"

"Twink's story, the real one, the one she told herself."

"She really did?" Harry asked.

"In a way. She ditched 'Caroline' in favor of autobiography. Daddy's last summer, Twink dictated this to him."

Harry reached up for the paper as Whizzer reached down to give him a quick kiss on the cheek. Harry blushed.

"I'm only the fastest thing on two legs, Harry," Whizzer said, jostling his shoulder with her knee. "My time for the hundred-yard dash is still a public school record for the fourth grade. Night."

She walked into the study, turned on the lights, and closed the door.

As Harry unfolded the piece of paper he held in his hand, he remembered something that made him uneasy. He hadn't touched Twink at all that day, not even to hold her hand or to kiss her forehead when he left.

127

## Other SIGNET Titles You Will Enjoy

☐ **LISTEN TO THE SILENCE by David W. Elliott.** A total and unique experience—gripping, poignant, most often, shattering. A fourteen-year-old boy narrates the chronicle of events that lead him into, through, and out of an insane asylum. "Each page has the ring of unmistakable truth . . . a well-written, tour de force, another Snake Pit . . ."—The New York Times Book Review.
(#Q4513—95¢)

☐ **THE AUTOBIOGRAPHY OF A SCHIZOPHRENIC GIRL by Marguerite Sechehaye.** The classic case history of a young girl who retreats completely into a world of fantasy, and her slow recovery. (#T4117—75¢)

☐ **ONE FLEW OVER THE CUCKOO'S NEST by Ken Kesey.** A powerful, brilliant novel about a boisterous rebel who swaggers into the ward of a mental institution and takes over. (#Q4171—95¢)

☐ **THE BETTER PART by Kit Reed.** A moving story about a young girl brought up in a correctional home and her coming of age. (#T4241—75¢)